Acting Edition

Legacy of Light

by Karen Zacarías

FOR PRODUCTION INQUIRIES

UNITED STATES AND CANADA
info@concordtheatricals.com
1-866-979-0447

UNITED KINGDOM AND EUROPE
licensing@concordtheatricals.co.uk
020-7054-7298

Each title is subject to availability from Concord Theatricals Corp.,
depending upon country of performance. Please be aware that
LEGACY OF LIGHT may not be licensed by Concord Theatricals Corp.
in your territory. Professional and amateur producers should contact
the nearest Concord Theatricals Corp. office or licensing partner to
verify availability.

LEGACY OF LIGHT was originally commissioned by the Arena Stage in Washington D.C.; Molly Smith, Artistic Director, Stephen Richard, Executive Director, and premiered on May 8th, 2009. The performance was directed by Molly Smith, with sets by Marjorie Bradley Kellogg, costumes by Linda Cho, lighting design by Michael Gilliam, souza design/composition by Andre J. Pluess, and dramaturgy by Jocelyn Clarke. The Stage Manager was Susan R. White. The cast was as follows:

EMILIE DU CHÂTELET. . . . . .Lise Bruneau
VOLTAIRE. . . . . Stephen Schnetzer
SAINT-LAMBERT/LEWIS. . . . . David Covington
OLIVIA/WET NURSE. . . . . Carla Harting
MILLIE/PAULINE . . . . Lindsey Kyler
PETER/MARQUIS DU CHÂTELET . . . . Michael Russotto

LEGACY OF LIGHT had its premiere on the west coast at the San Jose Repertory theater on March 24, 2011. The performance was directed by Kristen Brand, with fight direction by Dave Maier, sets by William Bloodgood, costumes by Brandin Baron, and sound design/composition by Jeff Mockus. The cast was as follows:

EMILIE DU CHÂTELET. . . . . Rachel Harker
VOLTAIRE. . . . . .Robert Yacko
SAINT-LAMBERT/LEWIS. . . . . .Miles Gaston Villanueva
OLIVIA/WET NURSE. . . . . Carrie Paff
MILLIE/PAULINE . . . . .Kathryn Tkel
PETER/MARQUIS DU CHÂTELET . . . . .Mike Ryan

CHARACTERS

EMILIE DU CHÂTELET – Beautiful intelligent woman. A scientist. Age forty-two.

VOLTAIRE – Emilie's lover; a playwright, philosopher, and scientist-wannabe. Age fifty-four.

SAINT-LAMBERT – Emilie's handsome younger lover. Also plays **LEWIS** – Age twenty-five.

OLIVIA – Modern professional woman. A scientist. Age forty-two. Also plays **WET NURSE.**

MILLIE – Modern twenty-one-year-old woman. An aspiring fashion designer. Also plays **PAULINE.**

PETER – Olivia's husband. Age forty-four. Also plays **MARQUIS DU CHÂTELET.**

SETTING

The set is simple and abstract.

The play should never stop because of the set.

Furniture that works in both eras.

An apple tree.

Light

and some darkness too.

And the fashion of the times.

TIME

FRANCE – Pre-Revolutionary 1700s.

NEW JERSEY – Now.

Many of Voltaire's actual quotations are peppered throughout the play.

ACT I

Scene One – Emilie's Room, France – 1700s

(**ST LAMBERT** *and* **EMILIE** *lie exhausted after passionate lovemaking.*)

SAINT LAMBERT. Incredible! What do you do to me, Emilie?

EMILIE. Jean Francois –

SAINT LAMBERT. My brow is still moist from the excitement.

EMILIE. The miracles of the body.

SAINT LAMBERT. Of your body, Madame.

(*He kisses* **EMILIE.**)

Feel my chest, it's about to burst with passion.

EMILIE. My dear poet, your heart is still beating quite fast.

SAINT LAMBERT. Thank goodness, I am young and strong.

EMILIE. Yes. Thank God for that.

(*They kiss again.*)

SAINT LAMBERT. I see stars when I kiss you.

EMILIE. Ah, don't tease me.

SAINT LAMBERT. My beautiful Lady Astronomer.

(*They kiss.*)

SAINT LAMBERT. Oh Emilie...

EMILIE. Jean-François.

SAINT LAMBERT. Emilie! The heat of your skin...the light of your eyes.

EMILIE. Mon cher, you are making me blush!

SAINT LAMBERT. Your blushing body is my universe.

(He kisses her neck.)

I came to the country to learn from a master. And yet, it was a mistress who taught me with the loveliest lessons.

EMILIE. And now the King has appointed you poet of his court.

SAINT LAMBERT. You will inspire every verse I write in Paris.

EMILIE. It's a pity you must leave tomorrow.

SAINT LAMBERT. If only we could keep the dawn at bay.

(He kisses her.)

I adore you...

EMILIE. Merci. Merci Beaucoup

SAINT LAMBERT. You are my Aphrodite!

EMILIE. *(Laughs.)* Oh, Jean-François!

SAINT LAMBERT. Emilie. Emilie –

VOLTAIRE. *(Offstage.)* Em-ilie!

(They stop.)

EMILIE. Oh no. Not now.

ST. LAMBERT. It's Voltaire! Voltaire!

EMILIE. Calm down.

ST LAMBERT. Voltaire! Voltaire is looking for you.

EMILIE. I will reason with him.

ST LAMBERT. Reason with Voltaire? About this?

(**VOLTAIRE** *opens the door and enters.*)

VOLTAIRE. Emilie!...St Lambert? Oh!!!

SAINT LAMBERT. Monsieur Voltaire!!!

EMILIE. Voltaire...my love.

VOLTAIRE. Good God! I cannot believe this!

EMILIE. Voltaire –

VOLTAIRE. You and Saint Lambert?

ST. LAMBERT. *Monsieur* Voltaire, I never meant –

EMILIE. Voltaire, calm down.

VOLTAIRE. Calm down? My heart is breaking. My soul recoils. Madame, you told me you were in your room, occupied with scientific experiments!

EMILIE. Voltaire, please!

VOLTAIRE. Instead I find you very occupied...with my pupil.

SAINT LAMBERT. Pardon me, *Monsieur.* I can only imagine how this must look.

VOLTAIRE. I see the woman I most adore betraying me for the carnal pleasure of...of...a PUPPY!

EMILIE. Voltaire!

ST LAMBERT. Monsieur! Hence you forget, I am a man with a title.

VOLTAIRE. That does not entitle you to court my lady!

EMILIE. Voltaire –

VOLTAIRE. Imagine what your husband would say about this, *Madame*?

EMILIE. Do not bring the *Marquis* into this discussion. This is between you and me. *Entre nous.*

VOLTAIRE. St. Lambert, you came here to learn from me. I have endured your insufferable arrogance and your inferior verse. And how do you repay me? You steal my muse.

EMILIE. Voltaire, really –

VOLTAIRE. I demand satisfaction.

EMILIE. What?!

ST LAMBERT. Do you wish to fight?

VOLTAIRE. If your swordplay is a deft as your wordplay, then most certainly.

> (**ST. LAMBERT** *draws his sword.*)

EMILIE. Voltaire you abhor violence!

> (**VOLTAIRE** *draws his sword.*)

ST. LAMBERT. You are a man of a certain ripe age, Monsieur.

VOLTAIRE. And you're not yet the ripe age of a man.

EMILIE. You must stop this.

ST LAMBERT. *En garde!*

VOLTAIRE. I have been imprisoned in the Bastille, banished to England, and had my plays produced at the Comedie Française. I have no fear. En garde.

> (*They begin to fight.*)

EMILIE. *Oh, ce n'est pas possible!*

ST. LAMBERT. Beware, *Monsieur* Voltaire, for I am a highly trained fighter.

VOLTAIRE. Beware, St. Lambert, for I am a highly trained thinker.

(He does something clever to avoid the blade.)

EMILIE. Then think, Voltaire! You could get hurt or killed!

VOLTAIRE. Then they will say I died for love.

(Still fighting.)

EMILIE. No, they will say you died for your pride and vanity.

VOLTAIRE. Fine, that too.

*(**ST. LAMBERT** almost strikes **VOLTAIRE**.)*

EMILIE. Careful! *Jean-François*, don't hurt him...

ST. LAMBERT. He attacks me! I must respond.

EMILIE. This is madness.

VOLTAIRE. *Au contraire,* see how courtly and civilized we are?

EMILIE. You are primitive and stupid.

ST. LAMBERT. *Voilá.*

VOLTAIRE. Oh!

EMILIE. You'll do anything for attention, even if it harms you.

VOLTAIRE. HA!

ST. LAMBERT. HA!

EMILIE. HA HA on you both.

*(**EMILIE** has grabbed her sword and deftly disarms or separates both men.)*

Let us act like rational thinking beings, shall we?

VOLTAIRE. First, I need to breathe.

ST LAMBERT. You know *Monsieu*r Voltaire, I am a great admirer of your poems and plays.

VOLTAIRE. Of course you are.

EMILIE. Perhaps we should give Voltaire some room to catch his breath, *mon cher*. Perhaps you should go for a walk –

ST. LAMBERT. And get some fresh air!

EMILIE. Thank you, my love.

> (**EMILIE** *kisses* **ST. LAMBERT.**)

> (**ST. LAMBERT** *gives* **VOLTAIRE** *a slight awkward bow.*)

ST. LAMBERT. *Monsieur* Voltaire –

> (**ST. LAMBERT** *exits.*)

EMILIE. Are you all right?

VOLTAIRE. No! I'm not all right! My heart is breaking!

EMILIE. Breathe.

VOLTAIRE. Saint Lambert?

EMILIE. Breathe.

VOLTAIRE. Saint Lambert!!

EMILIE. Breathe.

VOLTAIRE. SAINT LAMBERT!!!!!

EMILIE. Calm down.

VOLTAIRE. You replace me...with him? With that little puppy!

EMILIE. He is handsome; he is young.

VOLTAIRE. Poison daggers are piercing my bleeding heart.

EMILIE. Enough theatrics. You are being unreasonable and unjust.

VOLTAIRE. Emilie, my entire life is dedicated to reason and justice.

EMILIE. Then treat my behavior with the same fair tenderness you treat your own. I know about the other ladies in your life.

VOLTAIRE. I beg your pardon?

EMILIE. Your letters to them are beautiful.

(She pulls some letters out of her desk.)

VOLTAIRE. *(Beat.)* Who sent them to you?

EMILIE. An anonymous "friend" who wants to harm you and make me feel like a fool. And this is why I continue to tell you, my love, be careful of what you write...people are using everything you pen in an effort to harm you. To banish you. Good God, it's a constant battle having to protect you from yourself.

VOLTAIRE. Why didn't you say anything to me?

EMILIE. I will not beg any man to love me. Not even you.

VOLTAIRE. Forgive me, Emilie.

EMILIE. Remember how it was with us in the beginning? The passionate nights without sleep, the stolen kisses in dark hallways, the long fiery talks?

VOLTAIRE. Yes...I do.

EMILIE. Being with you is like being filled with light. With possibility.

VOLTAIRE. Our souls were made for each other.

EMILIE. Then forgive me and forgive Saint-Lambert for I'm certain he'd rather not be the man who stabbed France's favorite poet.

VOLTAIRE. We are all full of weakness and errors, let us mutually pardon each other our follies. It is the first law of nature.

EMILIE. Who would have imagined the first law of nature would be forgiveness? I would have thought the first law of nature would be change.

Scene Two

*(**PETER** enters his home with a grocery bag.)*

(He sings a popular rock and roll song about science...like the one by Thomas Dolby...or one by Sam Cooke*.)

*(He turns on the light. **OLIVIA** is sitting on the couch with a box on her lap.)*

PETER. Good Heavens, Olivia! You scared me!

OLIVIA. Sorry.

PETER. What are you doing sitting here alone in the dark?

OLIVIA. Nothing. Just thinking. You were singing our song!

PETER. Was I?

OLIVIA. I could have gone to the grocery store.

PETER. You haven't been to the grocery store in seven years.

OLIVIA. True.

PETER. And you're never home this early.

OLIVIA. I know. Always at work.

PETER. Is everything OK? You seem...

---

* A license to produce *Legacy of Light* does not include a performance license for a Thomas Dolby or Sam Cooke song. The publisher and author suggest that the licensee contact ASCAP or BMI to ascertain the music publisher and contact such music publisher to license or acquire permission for performance of the song. If a license or permission is unattainable for a Thomas Dolby or Sam Cooke song, the licensee may not use the song in *Legacy of Light* but should create an original composition in a similar style or use a similar song in the public domain. For further information, please see the Music and Third-Party Materials Use Note on page iii.

OLIVIA. I'm what?

PETER. You seem a little dazed.

OLIVIA. Dazed. Yes. But very happy.

PETER. Really?

OLIVIA. Yes. Really. How was your day?

PETER. Well, the school finally got those little pencils I ordered and Billy was able to grip one correctly. And suddenly his scrawls turned into legible letters. Billy wrote the best letter B ever. Three months of struggling and then today. He did it.

OLIVIA. So today is the day Billy writes his name.

PETER. Amazing that something as simple as a pencil can make a difference, you know.

OLIVIA. I think it is more than that. I think you are paying attention.

PETER. Well, yes, maybe.

OLIVIA. I've been paying attention too. *(Beat.)* Peter, I think I found it.

PETER. Found it? Olivia...

(She brings out a photograph.)

OLIVIA. My team wants to be very careful before an announcement is made...but I have every reason to believe I've discovered...the first evidence of a planet in formation.

PETER. A planet in formation. Where?

OLIVIA. See that little, little dot?

PETER. Barely...

OLIVIA. That's it. It's beyond our solar system...but not too far away...it orbits the blue star Vega. Of course the possibility that it might be a brown dwarf can't be entirely ruled out – but our calculations of its trajectory, its color, its temperature, the way it moves, of the proximity of a stellar nursery. If my hypothesis is correct...This is the embryonic core of a planet.

PETER. Olivia!

OLIVIA. I've named her Vega-B.

PETER. It has a name? This is huge!

OLIVIA. This is everything I've ever wanted.

PETER. Olivia, you are going to win a Nobel Prize.

OLIVIA. Peter, only two women have ever won the Nobel Prize in Physics.

PETER. You are going to be the third. First Billy, now this. Unbelievable.

OLIVIA. Now, we have to continue to observe, measure, calculate and predict...and wait to see if it's correct.

PETER. Wait? How long?!!!

OLIVIA. Oh...a million years, depending

PETER. Olivia, that's a long time.

OLIVIA. To us. But to the universe, it's nothing. *(Beat. Looks at the photograph.)*

By the way. I totaled the car.

PETER. What?

OLIVIA. Smashed. I wasn't paying attention.

PETER. What? Are you OK?

OLIVIA. Just five stitches.

PETER. Where?

OLIVIA. Here. You can't see because of my hair. They wanted to shave it. Can you believe it? They wanted to shave my hair. After all I've done to grow it out. But I urged them otherwise. I can be persuasive that way.

PETER. Totally totaled?

OLIVIA. Yes.

PETER. Why didn't you call me?

OLIVIA. Because I wanted to surprise you.

PETER. Surprise me more?

OLIVIA. I had to buy you something. I took a taxi. Then I walked home.

> *(She hands him a gift she pulls out of her bag.)*

Open it. It's for you.

PETER. You hate shopping.

OLIVIA. I know. Open it.

PETER. What is it?

OLIVIA. It's something you truly want, but do not have.

PETER. A wristwatch walkie talkie?

OLIVIA. Open it.

> *(**PETER** does. He pulls out some baby booties.)*

PETER. Oh.

OLIVIA. For you.

PETER. *(Beat.)* A little small, don't you think?

OLIVIA. I want to have a baby.

PETER. *(Beat.)* Oh, Olivia...

OLIVIA. Start where we stopped...

PETER. Olivia...sweetie...the baby part might have already passed us by.

OLIVIA. No! Don't say that. No. It hasn't…

PETER. I thought we made our peace with it.

OLIVIA. Peace?

PETER. I have my students. You have your work. We have our friends.

OLIVIA. I changed my mind. I don't want peace. I want a noisy, kicking, burping child.

PETER. Olivia, sweetie, there are certain facts…

OLIVIA. Facts! I know the facts. But facts are…fixed…they aren't knowledge. And I know…in my profession, that if you just look at an equation, a problem long enough, and do the math in your head, and dream about it…and focus…suddenly, when you least expect it…the perspective will shift…and light will shine and you will see a way.

PETER. And that's what happened to you today?

OLIVIA. The car was spinning and the metal was compressing and the glass was breaking, I had this still moment…and I conceived an idea.

(He hugs her and kisses her head.)

Peter, think about it. If a galaxy can have a baby, why can't we?

Scene Three

(**VOLTAIRE** and **EMILIE** address the audience.)

VOLTAIRE. Before we go much further, I think we should introduce ourselves.

EMILIE. Oh Voltaire, everyone knows who you are.

VOLTAIRE. Oh, look at them! They think they know, but do they really?

EMILIE. Everyone, this is Voltaire, the poet –

VOLTAIRE. The playwright –

EMILIE. And my lover. As the most celebrated philosopher of our time...

VOLTAIRE. And also the most persecuted.

EMILIE. Voltaire is something entirely new and wondrous.

VOLTAIRE. I am a self-made man.

EMILIE. His accomplishments are great and yet to many, he is a dire threat to our society.

VOLTAIRE. "Stand upright, speak thy thoughts: They only live who dare."

EMILIE. Voltaire and I fell in love over our mutual admiration of the English astronomer and mathematician Isaac Newton.

VOLTAIRE. Who would think the simple act of looking at an apple would suddenly birth a whole new way of thinking about the universe?

EMILIE. The knowledge and temptation of apples.

VOLTAIRE. Apples are my favorite fruit!

(**VOLTAIRE** pulls out an apple and bites into it.)

EMILIE. You know the wonderful story about the apple falling on Newton's head?

VOLTAIRE. I wrote it!

EMILIE. Yes! Voltaire wrote it! Voltaire made it up!

VOLTAIRE. Emilie! I did not make it up! During my exile in England, Newton told me that amazing story himself.

EMILIE. I've read and translated Newton's writings and nowhere in his notes does he mention apples. *(Beat.)*

VOLTAIRE. I met Emilie in 1733. I was thirty-eight.

EMILIE. I was twenty-six and married to the Marquis du Châtelet.

VOLTAIRE. A very understanding man, the Marquis.

EMILIE. Yes. My husband is very accepting of my eccentric nature to learn and to live with Voltaire in our house at Cirey...and I am very accepting of his distant battles and his many mistresses.

VOLTAIRE. We are French.

How could I not fall in love with her restless inquisitive mind? Besides, the love making: absolutely wonderful!

EMILIE. Delicious.

VOLTAIRE. She likes all sorts of experiments...I mean the curiosity of this woman...

EMILIE. *Si vous plait!*

VOLTAIRE. Together we worked on some of Newton's scientific theories. In 1736 we published *The Elements Of Newton*, where Emile worked out the pull of gravity on Saturn.

EMILIE. I used calculus to determine how gravity would feel on that planet.

VOLTAIRE. Her calculations filled pages and boggled my mind.

EMILIE. The book is under Voltaire's name...but dedicated to me.

VOLTAIRE. You were thrilled by the dedication I wrote.

EMILIE. I was...

VOLTAIRE. *(Beat.)* I think that is all you need to know about us?

EMILIE. I think there is one important detail that must be discussed. Don't you think?

VOLTAIRE. Oh that? They don't need to know that.

EMILIE. Yes, they do. *(Beat.)* We are dead. Dead and gone.

VOLTAIRE. I am not gone! I am the father of the Enlightenment. None of you would be sitting here as comfortably challenged and freely aware as you are if it wasn't for me?

EMILIE. We do take you for granted sometimes, don't we?

VOLTAIRE. The Declaration of Independence, the basis of your American Constitution grew from the seed of my thinking.

EMILIE. "I do not agree with what you have to say, but I'll defend to the death your right to say it."

VOLTAIRE. That famous line...I wrote that!

EMILIE. Voltaire, do any of these people know about my work?

VOLTAIRE. Your French translation of Newton's Principia was discovered and published under your name ten years after your death. And I wrote a dedication "Her memory is treasured by all who knew her intimately, and who were capable of perceiving the breadth of her mind."

EMILIE. *(Touched.) Merci, mon cher.*

> (**EMILIE** *kisses* **VOLTAIRE.**)

We've been dead for a long time, haven't we?

VOLTAIRE. Oh, not that long.

EMILIE. If my calculations are correct, I died over two hundred and seventy years ago.

VOLTAIRE. She was always better with numbers.

Scene Four

(**PETER** and **OLIVIA** meet **MILLIE**.)

MILLIE. Hi. I'm Millie

PETER. Thank you for meeting with us. I'm Peter.

OLIVIA. I'm Olivia. I like your hat.

MILLIE. I made it.

OLIVIA. It's stellar

MILLIE. You're the astrophysicist.

OLIVIA. Most people assume Peter is the scientist.

MILLIE. I don't understand what you do. But I think it must be amazingly amazing.

OLIVIA. I used to study dark matter. But I got tired of trying to know the unknowable. Now, I study the formation of planets.

MILLIE. The formation of planets. Wow!

PETER. Olivia is a tenured scientist at the Department of Terrestrial Magnetism at the Isaac Newton Institute. The first and only woman to have a tenured senior science position there.

MILLIE. And you are the teacher?

PETER. Yes, I teach elementary school. You work at the library.

MILLIE. I like books.

PETER. I do too.

MILLIE. But I'm not a librarian. You need a degree in library sciences to be a librarian. I'm still undegreed.

PETER. So what do they call you at work?

MILLIE. Millie, the book stacker. So, you want to have a baby?

OLIVIA. You're direct. I like that.

PETER. Yes. We want to have a baby.

OLIVIA. We always assumed a baby would come. But we got so busy.

PETER. Olivia's work is very demanding.

OLIVIA. Stars can be that way sometimes. And Peter...well helping to build a charter school...raising money...doing educational research. It's also a demanding job.

PETER. Fulfilling.

OLIVIA. Yes, fulfilling. We love our work. But suddenly I was almost forty.

PETER. How did we get to forty so fast?

OLIVIA. I feel young.

PETER. You look young.

OLIVIA. Thanks. But a body doesn't lie. We tried to get pregnant. And nothing happened.

PETER. We got tested.

OLIVIA. It turned out Peter had a low sperm count.

PETER. Not a low sperm count...a lower than average...

OLIVIA. Sorry, a lower than average sperm count. But that wasn't the problem.

The problem was me.

PETER. It wasn't you. It was the Cancer.

OLIVIA. Late-stage ovarian cancer.

MILLIE. Oh dear.

PETER. It was terrible.

OLIVIA. I think it was almost worse for you than for me. Peter took very good care of me.

PETER. I was worried sick. I screamed. I cried. I prayed.

OLIVIA. I just focused. I paid attention.

PETER. You have to be focused to survive late-stage ovarian cancer.

MILLIE. Focused...and very lucky.

OLIVIA. I've been in remission for a year.

PETER. And she, we want to start where we stopped.

OLIVIA. Although clearly, I cannot be part of it.

(Pause.)

MILLIE. But I can. *(Beat.)* Anyway, here are the medical forms you requested. And the background check from the police station. I was hoping you would call. So, I prepared.

OLIVIA. Your essay was beautiful.

MILLIE. Thank you.

(Pause.)

Anyway, I brought some things from my scrap book. So you can get to know me and my family a little. To help you with your choice.

PETER. This is great.

MILLIE. This is my brother Lewis. He is twenty-three, and two years older than me. He has a degree in computer science. He started a little IT company out of our Mother's house.

OLIVIA. He is very handsome!

MILLIE. And he has no idea. Here is a book report I wrote in fifth grade. I thought you might both like it.

PETER. A book report on Jack London's *To Build A Fire* by Emilia Montenaro.

MILLIE. Everyone calls me Millie, except my Mom.

PETER. "It is dumb to build a fire under a branch of ice. Everyone knows that fire is heat, light, oxygen and carbon monoxide. And ice is crystallized water sensitive to heat. Everyone except the stupid cold hunter. The end."

OLIVIA. A nice English-Science mix.

MILLIE. And this is a picture of my Dad. He was a pilot; he flew off with a flight attendant when I was three.

OLIVIA. Montenaro. He doesn't look Italian.

MILLIE. Montenaro is my Mom's family name. And this is my Mom.

OLIVIA. She's beautiful, like you.

MILLIE. Thank you.

PETER. She's so young.

MILLIE. Forty-four.

OLIVIA. What does she do?

MILLIE. She died a year ago.

OLIVIA. Oh, I'm sorry.

MILLIE. She was caught in a storm and hit by lightning.

OLIVIA. That's horrible.

MILLIE. It turns out that lightning is the natural force that kills the most people per year in the U.S.

PETER. I didn't know that.

OLIVIA. Our telescope gets hit by lightning hundreds of times a year.

MILLIE. Lewis was living at home with her when this all happened and I left school to help him with everything. We inherited the house and all that comes with that.

PETER. You are going to go back to school, aren't you?

MILLIE. Yes! *(Beat.)* But not back to college. I want to go to another school.

PETER. Another school?

MILLIE. There's a fashion design school...in Paris.

PETER. Paris!

MILLIE. They take ten students a year...and...

OLIVIA. You are one of them.

MILLIE. Imagine...me designing hats in Paris!

OLIVIA. Sounds like happiness.

PETER. And that's why you want to do this?

MILLIE. I've been thinking about this for a long time. I could help you, I could help myself, I could have your baby. I'm not ready to be a mother...but I am curious about being pregnant. I mean...a nine-month investment could change the world...for all of us. Life is short. I want to do something that matters.

OLIVIA. I like you.

MILLIE. I like you too.

OLIVIA. If we decide to move ahead with the plan, then we must establish that you are entering this agreement of your own free will for a total fee of twenty-eight thousand dollars.

PETER. And as the biological mother to this child, the state of New Jersey recognizes that this is your body and it's your right to terminate the pregnancy or refuse to give up the baby at birth.

MILLIE. I do. But I would be having this baby for you.

OLIVIA. Millie, do you think you could turn me into a mother?

MILLIE. No, but your baby will turn you into a mother. And I will help you have your baby.

> (**OLIVIA** *sighs.*)

I am interviewing five other couples. But I want you to be the parents.

PETER & OLIVIA. You do?

MILLIE. I know I don't fit the perfect profile of a "preferred surrogate mother."

I'm not married. I don't have kids. I don't have a full college education.

OLIVIA. Yes.

MILLIE. I've suffered the loss of my mother.

PETER. Yes.

MILLIE. But I'm smart.

OLIVIA. Yes.

MILLIE. And I'm healthy.

PETER. Yes.

MILLIE. And you like me.

PETER & OLIVIA. Yes.

PETER. We still have six interviews set up.

OLIVIA. What shall we do?

MILLIE. It's a big decision. Whoever you choose, her egg will become half of your child.

You have to be meticulous...and rational...and careful.

So interview all the preferred fertile women you want.

And then: choose me.

Scene Five – France 1700s

(**ST LAMBERT** *and* **EMILIE** *walking outside.*)

EMILIE. I have missed you, *Jean François.*

ST. LAMBERT. And I you.

EMILIE. The King is pleased with your poetry?

ST LAMBERT. He and the Queen are charmed.

EMILIE. They are not the only ones.

ST. LAMBERT. Yes...in fact, I had to beg His Royal Highness to have this time with you. He was resistant but I insisted.

EMILIE. You can be very persuasive.

ST. LAMBERT. But I must return to Paris tomorrow.

EMILIE. Tomorrow...but it's a day's journey and you just arrived.

ST. LAMBERT. I know. But the gardens of Versailles are in full bloom and the King does not want me to miss a moment of inspiration in capturing their beauty in verse.

EMILIE. I thought you would be staying until the end of the month.

ST. LAMBERT. My sole consolation is that your beauty blossoms every season, petals like yours never die.

EMILIE. But only one night!

ST LAMBERT. And so much can happen in one night...unless of course Voltaire is planning on interrupting us again.

EMILIE. He is in rehearsal. He is punishing me by banning me from his play and having my daughter Pauline read all the female roles aloud.

ST. LAMBERT. Good...so I can cast you all to myself.

EMILIE. I thought we would have more time together.

(*He starts to kiss her arm.*)

Oh *Jean-François*...Please...

ST. LAMBERT. To please is my command.

EMILIE. I have something that I must discuss with you now...

ST. LAMBERT. What should we discuss? Your wrist? Your arm? Your neck?

EMILIE. *Jean-François*, I am expecting.

ST. LAMBERT. Expecting?

EMILIE. I'm with child

ST. LAMBERT. I can't believe it.

EMILIE. Believe me, neither can I.

ST. LAMBERT. You are forty-two years old!

EMILIE. I know.

ST. LAMBERT. I thought...

EMILIE. I didn't think...

ST. LAMBERT. And yet...

EMILIE. Yes! You would think that by now...I would know better and...

ST. LAMBERT. And yet you are certain?

EMILIE. I'm afraid so. I am expecting your baby.

ST. LAMBERT. It's a miracle!

EMILIE. A miracle?

ST LAMBERT. Yes!

EMILIE. You are pleased?

ST. LAMBERT. Of course. You are having my child. Maybe a son!

EMILIE. Perhaps it will be a boy.

ST LAMBERT. Maybe he will look like me!

EMILIE. Perhaps he will.

ST. LAMBERT. This is so thrilling! A part of me is growing inside of you. Maybe our son will be a poet!

EMILIE. Or our daughter a scientist!

ST LAMBERT. I've never seen a woman look more beautiful than you do now. Your breasts are full, your face is glowing. *(He kisses her.)* You have made me a very happy man.

EMILIE. Oh, Jean-François, this is madness!

ST. LAMBERT. But I love you. I love you. *(He kisses her all over.)*

EMILIE. Please! Listen!

ST LAMBERT. You are so beautiful.

EMILIE. My condition presents certain difficulties.

ST. LAMBERT. Marquis du Châtelet and Monsieur Voltaire cannot deny what we have.

EMILIE. Having a baby now...

ST. LAMBERT. Is a gift from God! We have created a new soul for the world and nothing else matters. So trust the heavens and embrace fate. All is in the hands of providence.

EMILIE. Providence.

ST. LAMBERT. All is for the best, is it not?

EMILIE. Yes. All is for the best in this best of all possible worlds.

(*Enter* **VOLTAIRE** *and* **PAULINE**.)

PAULINE. *Bonsoir Maman. St Lambert.*

ST. LAMBERT. *Bonsoir!*

EMILIE. *Bonsoir* Pauline, Voltaire

ST LAMBERT. Mademoiselle. Monsieur Voltaire.

PAULINE. Are we interrupting you?

ST LAMBERT. No. No. Please join us, we were just talking.

VOLTAIRE. About what?

EMILIE. How was rehearsal, my dear Pauline?

PAULINE. Splendid!

ST. LAMBERT. Emilie tells me you are working on an extraordinary play.

VOLTAIRE. How does she know it is extraordinary if she hasn't been allowed to read it?

ST. LAMBERT. Ah, but she knows you, Monsieur.

PAULINE. I am making all the costumes.

EMILIE. Again?

PAULINE. *Maman*, it's the best part!

VOLTAIRE. The best part? Oh really?

EMILIE. The best part, Pauline, is your role, I'm sure.

PAULINE. Voltaire has me reading the part of an aristocrat's wife who is unjustly punished and transformed into a mouse by a foolish King.

ST. LAMBERT. A foolish King?

EMILIE. Really Voltaire...is this wise?

VOLTAIRE. Wise, no. Correct, yes.

EMILIE. Voltaire, are you looking to be banished?

VOLTAIRE. Pauline is really quite talented.

PAULINE. Although if you ask me...being a free mouse is a better fortune than being a foolish man's wife.

VOLTAIRE. And there lies the comedy and the tragedy.

ST. LAMBERT. Most young girls I know are thrilled at the prospect of marriage.

EMILIE. Not Pauline.

PAULINE. Maman has promised to take me to the salons of Paris when I'm sixteen. And when I am eighteen, Maman will demand that the Sorbonne accept both of us as students.

ST. LAMBERT. You two will be the fall of men. Your beauties will distract the boys from their studies.

PAULINE. Well, then the boys shouldn't look at us.

EMILIE. Indeed. Pauline, just make sure you don't neglect your calculus.

VOLTAIRE. We must continue with our rehearsal. I am looking for a talking pig. Perhaps St. Lambert would like to play the role?

ST LAMBERT. Chewing your words is always a worthy meal...but I am afraid that I shall be returning to Paris.

VOLTAIRE. But you just got here. Emilie has been looking forward to your visit.

EMILIE. You heard him, Voltaire, *Jean-François* has important duties.

ST. LAMBERT. I am writing poems on the King's flowers.

VOLTAIRE. Ahh, tending another man's garden, I see.

EMILIE. Voltaire misses reciting his poetry at Court more than he cares to admit.

VOLTAIRE. It's their loss; the King said I was the best poet of the century.

EMILIE. Voltaire has a need to be admired by the very people he despises.

VOLTAIRE. Why yes, even St. Lambert likes my plays.

PAULINE. Maman, you look pale...do you feel all right?

EMILIE. I couldn't feel better, I'm fine, my dear. Perfect, really

(Cleary she is going to throw up. She exits.)

PAULINE. I will see to Maman.

*(***PAULINE*** exits.)*

ST. LAMBERT. Perhaps the supper disagreed with her.

VOLTAIRE. Or the puppy.

ST. LAMBERT. I am not a puppy.

VOLTAIRE. I would stay and debate that, but I must find another pig for my play.

Scene Eight

(**OLIVIA** *talks to the Board of Directors and Patrons of the Institute.*)

OLIVIA. Thank you, Tom. I should attend these dinners more often. Good evening, ladies and gentlemen, members of the board, patrons, and trustees of the Isaac Newton Institute. My name is Dr. Olivia Hasting Brown, and I am Senior Astrophysicist and Tenured Fellow in the Department of Terrestrial Magnetism.

Would you like to see a picture of my baby?

(*The room darkens. An image of a tiny dot or planet with gaseous particles.*)

What you are seeing might be the embryonic core of a planet. We don't know conclusively. We must and will continue to examine the data. But I hope what we see is what I think it is.

I have already named her Vega B.

So what do we know? Until the 1990s the only planets we knew were those in our solar system. Since then, our telescopes have gotten so powerful, we have now identified over five hundred worlds outside of our solar system.

And now I think we have just discovered our youngest planet yet.

So how was my embryonic planet Vega B created?

We know that planets are formed either from the debris of the birth of a new star or from the remains of a star that is dying. The "baby" planets spin, collide and coalesce over time, their gravity pulling debris to their core, spinning and growing, taking millions and millions of years.

OLIVIA. But I think my Vega B is following a very different path. I think a sudden gravitational collapse will allow her to obtain her planetary shape in a fraction of the time of other planets. My critics say that the turbulent winds created by the collapse will blow my fledgling planet away. But I hope, and believe, that the hurricane–like storms surrounding Vega-B will protect her and form a calm eye at the center that will allow the embryonic planet to accumulate debris and grow, despite the chaos around her.

I think there is more than one way to make a planet.

If I'm right and my embryo Vega B matures and condenses, she will become a real planet that might be fourteen times the size of Jupiter. Boy! That's a big planet!

I can't wait to see her grow up.

Scene Seven – New Jersey, Now

(**MILLIE** *is pinning* **LEWIS**'s *clothes. She is two months pregnant.*)

LEWIS. What do you mean you're pregnant?

MILLIE. Careful, Lewis, or I'm going to prick you.

LEWIS. Pregnant? Really?

MILLIE. Yes. You have to stand still or the cuffs will be uneven and your date will be ruined.

LEWIS. Ruining my date? What about ruining your life?

MILLIE. Do you know how long it's taken me to make this for you?

LEWIS. Don't we have enough problems? Mom's dead. My college loans. Your college loans. The possible foreclosure. The leaky roof. *(Pause.)* What are you going to do?

MILLIE. Do? Oh, I'm going to have it. Stand straight.

LEWIS. How can you have a boyfriend I don't know about?

MILLIE. I don't.

LEWIS. Is this some random hookup in the aisles of the supermarket or something?

MILLIE. No.

LEWIS. Then, who is the father?

MILLIE. Peter. And his wife, Olivia is going to be the Mother.

LEWIS. What? Who? Ouch!

MILLIE. You know that brilliant couple I told you about? Remember? I told you I wanted to help them.

LEWIS. The couple from Princeton? I thought you were going to be picking up their mail, and watering their plants.

MILLIE. I'm having their baby. I am a surrogate mother.

LEWIS. Did you have sex with this Peter guy?

MILLIE. No! It was by artificial insemination.

PETER. What?

MILLIE. It's my egg and Peter's sperm.

LEWIS. Where did you get such an idea?

MILLIE. At my local library.

LEWIS. Millie, what in the world have you gotten yourself mixed up in?

MILLIE. Lewis, it's all above board. They're paying me. There's a contract and a schedule.

LEWIS. They're paying you? They're buying your baby?

MILLIE. No, I'm being compensated for nine months of service.

LEWIS. Why are you doing this?

MILLIE. Because, Mr. Cyber analyst, we are thirty-five thousand dollars in debt and the bank is about to foreclose on our house. I'm stacking books and you're downstairs writing code but it's not enough. We are about to lose everything. I had to do something...big.

LEWIS. Big? This is huge. You are having a baby to save us from losing our home!?

MILLIE. I didn't tell Peter and Olivia that... It sounds unhealthy and desperate.

LEWIS. Because it is!!

MILLIE. Turn around.

LEWIS. What did you tell them?

MILLIE. They think they are helping me fulfill my lifelong dream of going to Paris

LEWIS. Paris? What would you possibly do in Paris?

MILLIE. Go to fashion design school.

LEWIS. And do what?

MILLIE. Design clothes?

LEWIS. At some expensive fancy pants Fashion School in Paris?

MILLIE. It's not called that. But yes.

LEWIS. And they believed you?

MILLIE. Yes.

LEWIS. Why Paris?

MILLIE. It's supposed to be so beautiful.

LEWIS. New Jersey is beautiful. It's the Garden State, for crying out loud. And we live in Maplewood which is very close to Mont Clair...and that's French enough if you ask me.

MILLIE. Lewis, calm down, I'm not going anywhere. I'm staying here and we are saving the house.

LEWIS. By giving away your baby? Ohmigod! Ohmigod! Omigod!

MILLIE. Who stood by me when I painted my hair green in ninth grade?

LEWIS. I did.

MILLIE. Who ate all my servings of bacon when I went through your pigs-are-too-smart-to-be-eaten stage?

LEWIS. I did.

MILLIE. Who wore a dark purple tuxedo shirt I made for his prom!

LEWIS. I did.

MILLIE. And you looked amazingly amazing.

LEWIS. I can't stand by you on this.

MILLIE. Why?

LEWIS. It's not right. You are giving away our flesh and blood. I am that baby's uncle. He's my nephew. It's our family DNA.

MILLIE. I know you and all your college buddies donated sperm for beer money.

LEWIS. It's not the same.

MILLIE. Oh really?

LEWIS. It's different for girls! You get, you know, pregnant. I'm your big brother. I am supposed to protect you.

MILLIE. From what?

LEWIS. From yourself, apparently.

MILLIE. I am very proud of what I am doing. This baby wouldn't exist without Peter and Olivia. They conceived this idea that will become a person! They are an amazingly amazing couple. Who need me. And they don't know, but we need them.

LEWIS. There are three laws of the universe: Pay your taxes. Wear a seatbelt. Keep your kin.

MILLIE. They chose me...because they liked me...because they saw a spark in me that they hope they will see in the eyes of their child. And why you don't think that's a tribute to Mom and us is beyond me.

LEWIS. Mom would be so mad!

MILLIE. Mom said we should always do something that matters.

LEWIS. They chose you because you are bright, sweet and trusting and...very blind when it comes to things like this.

MILLIE. Blind?

> (**LEWIS** *takes off his glasses and sets them up on a table or mantle.*)

LEWIS. You don't see the world as it really is! You and that baby are the only relatives I have left in this world. You are my only family. And without family, what are we? Nothing.

> (**LEWIS** *rips his suit off at the seams. Exasperated he exits.*)

MILLIE. I'm doing this to for us. Lewis, don't you see? I'm doing this for our family!

Scene Nine – France 1700s

(**VOLTAIRE** *is searching for something.* **EMILIE** *is daydreaming at her desk. She is four months pregnant.*)

EMILIE. They are right here, on the chair.

VOLTAIRE. Oh.

(**VOLTAIRE** *puts on the* **LEWIS** *glasses.*)

EMILIE. Am I right?

VOLTAIRE. Women always know where things are.

(**VOLTAIRE** *comes and oversees her work.*)

EMILIE. I'm trying to settle accounts and pay bills. But I am having trouble concentrating.

VOLTAIRE. That's because your breasts are growing.

EMILIE. You have a vivid imagination, my dear.

VOLTAIRE. Your breasts are growing.

EMILIE. Your ability to measure is something I question.

VOLTAIRE. That was uncalled for.

EMILIE. I apologize.

VOLTAIRE. You know that was a humiliating episode in our history.

EMILIE. All you have accomplished, and this still bothers you?

VOLTAIRE. You should have told me you were performing your OWN calculations at night.

EMILIE. I didn't think it would matter. And did I not spend all day with you, helping you in your scientific quest?

VOLTAIRE. It makes me ill just thinking about it.

EMILIE. I tried to tell you that your measurements were off!

VOLTAIRE. I KNOW! You could have told me that you were entering the same science competition as I was!

EMILIE. I didn't know my experiment would work.

VOLTAIRE. Everyone knows you should have won the Academie's Science Prize.

EMILIE. I was happy with my commendation.

VOLTAIRE. I wasn't. I wanted to win.

EMILIE. Well, our expectations are very different, aren't they?

VOLTAIRE. What is wrong with you? You are fierce and savage tonight.

[handwritten: insulting instead of accepting / less/demeaning]

EMILIE. Forgive me, I am tired.

VOLTAIRE. But your books are all stacked carefully; you haven't touched your telescope in days.

EMILIE. I've been paying bills, and the drapes and curtains need to be replaced, and the cook is late, and the horse fodder is low. If I were a man I'd...just get rid of all the useless things in my life

VOLTAIRE. Are you with child?

EMILIE. What?

VOLTAIRE. It's no longer a question. You are with child!

EMILIE. Judge a man by his questions, you always say.

VOLTAIRE. You are forty-two years old!

EMILIE. Is that a question or a statement?

VOLTAIRE. Do not walk away from me! Emilie, look at me.

EMILIE. I can't.

VOLTAIRE. You and I were lovers for more than a decade; not once did we jeopardize your health.

EMILIE. I know.

VOLTAIRE. You were bedridden for months after birthing your son. And it's a miracle you survived the birth of Pauline.

EMILIE. I know.

VOLTAIRE. Does Saint-Lambert know what you are risking?

EMILIE. No.

VOLTAIRE. I see.

EMILIE. I must ask my husband to leave his post and spend time with me. The child must at least appear to be his.

VOLTAIRE. I am sure he will be amenable.

EMILIE. Voltaire, I'm afraid.

VOLTAIRE. No. You are fearless, remember?

EMILIE. I will die in childbirth.

VOLTAIRE. Don't say that.

EMILIE. There is so much I want to do.

VOLTAIRE. *(Beat.)* I have heard there are ways...to provoke the bleeding. We should go to Paris tonight.

EMILIE. No.

VOLTAIRE. It might be your chance to live.

EMILIE. Or my chance to die sooner. Voltaire, I'm not prepared to die by tomorrow

VOLTAIRE. The odds are better than childbirth. It might be a risk worth taking.

EMILIE. Jean François called my pregnancy a miracle.

VOLTAIRE. Jean-François is a foolish boy, blind to the consequences of his actions.

EMILIE. I've started to have dreams about the baby.

VOLTAIRE. Emilie, be rational. This child could be the end of you.

EMILIE. I dreamt that this one would be a scientist, just like me.

VOLTAIRE. Stop.

EMILIE. And she will discover the secret of the skies and change the world.

VOLTAIRE. Emilie, I always thought it was you who would do that.

>   *(Beat.)*

EMILIE. I better get to work then. I have less than five months to do everything I need to do.

Scene Ten

(At the Waiting Room of a Doctor's Office.)

*(****PETER*** *and* ***MILLIE*** *look at a picture.* ***MILLIE*** *is about twelve weeks pregnant.)*

PETER. *(Wiping his eyes.)* I'm sorry. I don't know what came over me in there.

MILLIE. Crying is a very normal thing.

PETER. I mean, I knew there was a baby because well, your belly. But seeing it. Hearing it. It just became so real.

MILLIE. Very real.

PETER. *(Looks at the photo.)* He kind of looks like an alien, doesn't he?

MILLIE. I think he has your nose.

PETER. It could be a "she."

MILLIE. She might have your nose.

PETER. Do I have an alien nose?

MILLIE. I don't know. I've never seen an alien. But this is amazingly amazing.

*(****OLIVIA*** *runs in.)*

OLIVIA. Sorry. Sorry! I didn't mean to keep you waiting.

PETER. Olivia.

OLIVIA. Simply a crazed day at the lab. Some of the exponential numbers are not producing the results we were hoping; the color seems to be shifting, which could mean a drastic temperature change and the Mariah Mitchell Observatory is suddenly not as available. We might have to go to Hawaii to get use of the equipment there...is everything all right?

MILLIE. Oh yes.

OLIVIA. Great!...OK...so are we ready to go in and meet this baby?

> *(Beat.)*

PETER. We already did.

OLIVIA. You already did? You saw the baby already?

MILLIE. The appointment was an hour ago.

OLIVIA. I really didn't mean to be so late again.

MILLIE. We really tried to wait.

OLIVIA. The team meeting went on and on. And I lost track of time...

MILLIE. That happens.

PETER. This was the ultrasound, Olivia! The baby's first sonogram!

OLIVIA. I know.

PETER. Olivia, you have to do better. You have to focus on this. Now.

OLIVIA. Right. You're right. I promise, no matter what is happening in the universe, to never ever to be late again. I'm just trying to get as much work out of the way before the baby comes. Peter, Millie, I'm very sorry. Really! Nobody is more upset than me to have missed all this.

MILLIE. Look at the picture.

OLIVIA. Oh...well...so...there really is...something. A baby blob. *(Beat.)* An alien baby.

MILLIE. If you hold it like that...and squint, see? That's might be his nose. I think he has Peter's nose.

OLIVIA. So is he...a little boy?

MILLIE. We don't know. It's too early. But I can't wait to find out.

OLIVIA. No. Let's be old fashioned and not know.

PETER. What?

MILLIE. You aren't...curious?

PETER. I thought we agreed we were going to find out. So we could talk about names? So it would begin to feel... real for you?

OLIVIA. Agnes for my grandmother. George, after your father. Right?

PETER. You don't want to know?

OLIVIA. No. I don't want to know.

(**PETER** *starts to talk.*)

MILLIE. We will all find out soon enough, right?

PETER. Right.

OLIVIA. How did it feel? I want to know details.

MILLIE. They put this cold clear jelly on my belly...and then they turned on the ultrasound and stirred the stick and *voilá*. We could suddenly see inside.

OLIVIA. And how do you feel?

MILLIE. Really happy and a little scared.

PETER. We heard a fetal heartbeat.

OLIVIA. You did? How did it sound?

MILLIE. Loud and Fast.

OLIVIA. That's wonderful.

PETER. You'll hear it. Next time –

OLIVIA. Yes of course...next time.

MILLIE. Yes.

(Beat. Everyone starts to leave.)

OLIVIA. I really like your jacket.

MILLIE. Thank you. I made it.

OLIVIA. Here. *(**OLIVIA** hands **MILLIE** the picture.)*

MILLIE. Olivia...that's yours.

OLIVIA. Oh yes. Right. Mine. Thanks. The picture of the baby...my baby.

Scene Six – France 1700s

(**VOLTAIRE** *walks across the stage. He pulls out an apple...he is about to eat it. But he sees the audience.*)

VOLTAIRE. I know what you are thinking! I know what you are thinking! You feel betrayed by the Voltaire you know and love. You look at me and think "Oh-la-la, I thought the story about Isaac Newton and the apple was true." And now you might feel a little deceived. First, because you didn't know that story had anything to do with me. Second, because now you suspect I made it up.

I will tell you these two things:

UN: I did meet/see Sir Isaac Newton in England.

DEUX: There is an apple tree not too far from his house.

Newton's mathematical work proves that this is a rational universe that functions like clockwork. That, for every action, there is always an opposed and equal reaction; that an unmoving object won't move unless a force acts upon it; and that an object that is in motion will not stop unless a force acts upon it. He shows that the same force that works on a falling object on Earth, keeps the moon in orbit. And that the moon's gravity pulls our ocean tides. Newton proves that everything is connected...not by the superstitious beliefs of the Church or the unjust laws of the State or the cruel tyranny of the King...but by rational scientific cause and effect.

Everything is Cause and Effect.

"Nothing will change unless a force acts upon it."

His equations are not just equations for understanding the Universe, they offer a rational design for changing our world for the better. By understanding cause and effect, we suddenly have the light to see past fate and find the will to change our lives.

So! Perhaps I took a little poetic license! *Peut-être* the story about the apple is something I made up. But don't you see? I want the reach of Newton's ideas to be as simple and as common as an apple.

> (**VOLTAIRE** *bites or is about to bite into the apple when* **CHÂTELET** *walks on carrying a package.*)

CHÂTELET. Monsieur Voltaire!

VOLTAIRE. Marquis du Châtelet!

> (*The warmly shake hands.*)

CHÂTELET. I am pleased to see you.

VOLTAIRE. I know your wife appreciates your help and understanding.

CHÂTELET. Is Emilie in the house?

VOLTAIRE. Yes, with Pauline.

CHÂTELET. How is she feeling?

VOLTAIRE. She's working.

CHÂTELET. As always, that Emilie. I have a wonderful surprise for my daughter.

VOLTAIRE. Pauline will be thrilled to see you.

CHÂTELET. Enjoy your apple!

> (**VOLTAIRE** *and* **CHÂTELET** *walk offstage in (opposite) directions.*)

Scene Twelve

(**EMILIE** *is five months pregnant.*)

PAULINE. Papa! Maman! Maman! Papa is here! And he has brought a package!

(**CHÂTELET** *enters with a large package.*)

EMILIE. Florent!

CHÂTELET. Emilie!

(*They kiss each other's cheeks.*)

EMILIE. Thank you for coming so promptly.

CHÂTELET. I've been gone from home too long.

EMILIE. Is all well with you?

CHÂTELET. It's you I worry about.

EMILIE. I feel fine. I'm still working.

CHÂTELET. And what captivates the mind of Emilie these days?

EMILIE. I am translating Newton's geometry into calculus.

CHÂTELET. Good God? Why?

EMILIE. Because I think it will help clarify his ideas...and my questions.

CHÂTELET. Isaac Newton. Isaac Newton. You and Voltaire and that Isaac Newton. If you ask me, I think it's quite obvious that apples fall out of trees...that things that go up, come down.

PAULINE. Yes, how else would we make an apple tart?

EMILIE. Apples don't fall because they are apples. Pauline, haven't you done any of the calculus problems I gave you?

PAULINE. Oh, Maman, I've been too preoccupied with the pig costume.

CHÂTELET. The pig costume?

PAULINE. For Voltaire's play. Papa, you'll love it.

(*She pulls out the pig hat from the same cloth bag* **OLIVIA** *has.*)

See the ears? I attached string so they wiggle.

(**CHÂTELET** *laughs.*)

EMILIE. I spent a lot of time preparing those lessons for you.

PAULINE. Maman, they are just numbers, and numbers, will always be around. They are infinite.

CHÂTELET. Pauline! Pauline! Pauline! (*Still amused by her.*)

PAULINE. Papa, what is in the package?

PAPA. A gift for you.

PAULINE. Maman, did you hear? It's a gift for me. For me!

EMILIE. Pauline...

PAULINE. Can I open it?

CHÂTELET. Yes!

EMILIE. No!

PAULINE. (*Beat.*) Why?

EMILIE. I prefer she not know about that package, just yet.

CHÂTELET. But she'll love it.

PAULINE. Oh! And I can't un-know what I know. It's there, isn't it? I see it.

What is in it?

CHÂTELET. Open it, my little one. And find out.

(Beautiful, beautiful silvery white cloth.)

PAULINE. Oh Papa. Thank you! It's exquisite.

CHÂTELET. It's silk. The finest. Your mother told me that this was your favorite color.

PAULINE. It is! Look, Maman. Each strand is colored yet translucent. So much work. Feel it! Look at the weave…like stars.

EMILIE. I've never thought of cloth like that.

PAULINE. Thank you. Thank you. I'm almost afraid to cut it. But I have something I want to make. I've designed a bodice for Maman since she's getting so big. It ties under the belly.

EMILIE. Do not make anything for me. Not for me.

PAULINE. I know! I can make a dressing gown for the baby!

CHÂTELET. Pauline, I brought it just for you.

PAULINE. For me? Oh! What should I make with it?

EMILIE. Your wedding dress.

(Beat.)

PAULINE. NO! Maman…No!

EMILIE. Pauline.

PAULINE. You promised Paris, and the University –

EMILIE. I know…

CHÂTELET. Many young women marry at fifteen. This is not a terrible thing. You will thank us.

PAULINE. No! No! Voltaire will stop you! Voltaire!

VOLTAIRE. What is it?

PAULINE. Help me. It's Maman and Papa. They are making me marry.

VOLTAIRE. But you are too young. And too bright. And your mother promised –

EMILIE. Duke Fabio has accepted Marquis du Châtelet's dowry offer.

PAULINE. Duke Fabio!

VOLTAIRE. That old Italian who snored during my discourse on the Church and taxes?

EMILIE. He is kind. He is decent.

PAULINE. Duke Fabio is old. He has a sunken chest and no neck.

CHÂTELET. The Duke is a fine nobleman. He is a blood relation to the Pope. He owns a beautiful estate in Tuscany. You will want for nothing.

PAULINE. No! No! No! Maman, I don't want to live in Italy.

VOLTAIRE. Marriage is the only adventure open to the cowardly.

EMILIE. Voltaire, what do you know about marriage?

CHÂTELET. You are not a father. You cannot possibly understand!

EMILIE. Pauline if something should happen to me. If I die...

PAULINE. Papa –

CHÂTELET. I cannot bring a young girl to the barracks or a battlefield.

PAULINE. I could live with Voltaire! He has known me all my life!

VOLTAIRE. She could.

CHÂTELET. You have as many enemies as you have friends. If she lived here with you...

EMILIE. Tongues would wag. She would never be able to marry.

PAULINE. I never want to marry!

CHÂTELET. Fortunately, that is not for you to decide.

PAULINE. Voltaire, tell Maman this whole thing is ridiculous. Reason with her.

VOLTAIRE. It is ridiculous! And also, I'm afraid, true.

PAULINE. This is not fair.

CHÂTELET. This is the world we live in.

EMILIE. Pauline...please...you must marry the Duke.

PAULINE. You promised I could study and live with you!

EMILIE. Pauline, all is for the best in this best of all possible worlds.

PAULINE. Maman.

EMILIE. You must believe me. You must trust me.

PAULINE. A good mother should not harm her children

EMILIE. A good mother must prepare her children for the world.

PAULINE. One where mothers betray their daughters?

VOLTAIRE. Pauline –

PAULINE. I am your child!

CHÂTELET. Yes, *(Kisses her forehead.)* and, it's now time for you to grow up.

> *(He exits.)*

PAULINE. Tell me, Maman, why do apples fall?

(**EMILIE** *picks up and hands her the cloth.*)

I thought it was going to be different for me. I am your daughter.

EMILIE. Everything changes (*She strokes* **PAULINE***'s cheek.*) but you will always be my daughter.

(**EMILIE** *exits.*)

PAULINE. But why do apples fall? I'll listen this time, I promise.

(**VOLTAIRE** *consoles* **PAULINE** *in a parental way...maybe stroking her hair.*)

VOLTAIRE. Apples do not fall, Pauline. They are dragged down to the ground by a force.

(*Lights down on* **PAULINE** *and* **VOLTAIRE***. We watch a frantic* **OLIVIA***, walk rush down the stage. She is reading a book on pregnancy and devouring an apple, as her papers and pen falls. She scoops to pick them up, and continues at a fast pace, and finds the two pictures...one of the baby and one of her planet. She looks at them both.*)

Scene Eleven

EMILIE. The experiment...my first experiment started with light. Voltaire was entering a paper in the Science Academy Competition to discover the essence of fire. My role was to help him. He focused on heat. All day, I watched him measure the heat of metals, incorrectly, as it turned out. But at night, I would sit in the darkness...and think about another property of fire: light. Light...the properties of light.

Light comes from the sun at a terrific speed...faster and with more force than a cannon ball. In fact, when I sat down with my calculations, I concluded light must travel millions of meters per second. And yet, it does not destroy the Earth. All authorities at the time assumed that light had solid weight...but upon reflection, I realized that was impossible. The earth would not survive the pelting of light. If light had weight, it would destroy all life on the planet.

My conclusion: Light has no mass.

If light has no mass, then how does it heat?

    (A rainbow appears.)

Through its colors.

I set up thermometers side by side on the wall and I let a prism-burst-of-light shine on them to measure the heat of the different colors. As I watched the colors move across the thermometers, I discovered that the temperatures fluctuated with different colors. Then, I saw that the thermometer which had been recording the red part of the rainbow, that its temperature did not go down even though there was no light I could see shining on it. It was as if an invisible light, a color we could not see, was heating it.

Perhaps different colors carry different amounts of heat.

Perhaps there are more types of light beams than we can see with the naked eye.

Light we see heats and burns.

And strangely enough, the light we cannot see does the same.

It heats and burns – just like love.

> *(Beat and discovery.)*

Is it possible that Light and Love share the same properties? They must!

Love burns; different types of love carry different amounts of heat. And although we cannot see it, smell it, or touch it, we can feel love. It glows.

Love does not have weight! Love has no mass!

Otherwise, how would our souls survive the pelting?

> *(We see* **OLIVIA** *looking at the two pictures and* **PAULINE** *touching the material for her wedding dress.)*

End of Act I

ACT II

Scene One

OLIVIA. *(A school lecture.)* Hello Senior Girl Scout Troup three hundred twenty-one of Mont Clair, New Jersey! My name is Doctor Olivia Hasting Brown.

I am an astrophysicist.

My life's work is to study the universe.

For the next ninety minutes I will be giving you an overview of my work that will hopefully inspire bright young women such as yourselves to consider science as an exciting career path. Ready?

(She looks at her watch and realizes she is in trouble.)

Oh. I'm sorry, I'm so so sorry. I just now realized that I have a doctor's appointment scheduled in half and hour. And I really cannot be late. Really. I can't be late.

So instead of ninety minutes, I will give you a lecture that lasts two minutes...and at the end of the two minutes, you will know almost as much as I do.

Ready?

Let's start four hundred years ago, with the invention of the telescope. Where once we were blind, we could now see...and extend our vision up into the heavens... and to the worlds beyond our own. Galileo, the father of astronomy and modern science, declares the universe is written in the language of mathematics. Then Sir Isaac Newton drops an apple and infers that the same force that pulls the apple down to the earth, moves the planets, and describes a mechanical universe that runs as prim as a Puritan on a bicycle. Enter the Enlightenment, and an obscure female scientist Emilie du Chatelet throws a wrench in Newton's prim bicycle when she discovers that light has no mass and that energy does not disappear because...energy is mass times velocity squared. Einstein comes along and builds upon her work, suggesting that light travels in both particles and waves, that time is a malleable force, that energy is mass times the SPEED OF LIGHT SQUARED. Suddenly you have a more chaotic, volatile universe; not a Puritan on a bicycle, but a Hells Angel on a Harley. Throw in the fact that the universe is STILL expanding and you have a complex, interconnected Universe gunning on all cylinders and making one hell of a wheelie while barely respecting the dynamics of physical law.

OLIVIA. This is the universe we know.

Let me tell you what we don't know.

Dark Matter.

What is dark matter?

We have no earthly idea. Dr. Vera Rubin, a DC scientist and mother of four, proposed its existence it in the 1970s...and still we do not know what Dark Matter is – at all.

We think Dark Matter fills the emptiness of space. It is matter that is undetectable to our senses, reflects no light, and in fact, is beyond our entire electromagnetic spectrum. Dark matter makes up ninety percent of the universe. Everything we see: you, me, the supermarket, the planet, the cosmos: make up the other ten percent of the universe.

Everything else...is Dark Matter. It is the great unknown.

Dark Matter is floating in this room, through us, around us, like a ghostly presence we can't see, smell, or touch. But it's there: holding...binding our universe tight, generating all the gravity that keeps the galaxies from spinning out of control.

The truth is: We just don't know what Dark Matter is. In fact, we don't really know what Gravity is either.

The thing we know the least is holding us together the most.

That was two minutes. I hope you learned something. You know, every time we look at the night sky, we are looking at the past, seeing light from a star that may not exist anymore. But you are the future. And I hope that some of you young ladies will become scientists and carry the torch and shine light on everything we still do not yet know about the universe.

Because lately, the only thing I've learned is how very little I really know.

Thank you. Thank you very much.

> (**OLIVIA** *runs off. Perhaps* **EMILIE** *strolls by, very pregnant eating an apple and writing notes or reading a physics book.*)

Scene Two

(Millie and Lewis' house. **MILLIE** *is seven months pregnant. Perhaps there is water dripping from the ceiling...eventually a potted plant gets moved to absorb the water.)*

MILLIE. Four thousand dollars. That will pay off the property taxes. I've made a chart. The utilities are squared away. We almost paid off the months Mom didn't pay for the house. I have another eight thousand dollars coming that we can use to fix the roof, oh, and replace the shingles. Then, we can get our heads above water.

LEWIS. You made a chart? God. I don't know what to say.

MILLIE. You don't have to say anything. Nothing is fixed. We just have to focus and deal with one thing at a time.

LEWIS. But I can't focus on anything. This thing is making me not think straight. I'm useless.

MILLIE. Lewis, don't say things like that.

LEWIS. You know, I read on the internet that in India, some husbands force their wives to birth babies for rich couples to make ends meet.

MILLIE. That's horrible.

LEWIS. Isn't that what you are doing?

MILLIE. No. I reached this decision of my own free will, thank you very much. And it's about a lot more than just making ends meet.

God, I want to eat an apple with salt, RIGHT NOW. *(She gets an apple and eats it as she shakes salt on it.)*

Lewis, once we pay the taxes and we fight the foreclosure, we can then sell the house.

LEWIS. Sell our home?

MILLIE. If we sell the house...then we can be free.

LEWIS. Free?

MILLIE. To do things. To see the world. God, my ankles are as big as eggplants!

(*She sits and put her feet up.*)

LEWIS. Wait a minute. This is our family home. We grew up here. We inherited this. My business is in the basement.

MILLIE. But we both can't live here forever. And your computer deserves a room with windows, don't you think? Hand me a pillow, please.

(**MILLIE** *tucks it under her feet to keep them elevated.*)

LEWIS. Grandpa Montenaro came to this country with the dream of building a life here. He worked like a dog and died too soon. But Mom, she bought this house. She loved it.

MILLIE. She complained about it an awful lot.

LEWIS. But it was hers! Don't you see? This is our place in the world. Our past is this house. And my future, my dream, is here too! And you want to get rid of it? So you can fly off to Paris? To go to a school that would never admit you?

MILLIE. It sounds really bad when you say it like that.

LEWIS. Yeah! If we sell the house where would we live?

MILLIE. We could rent. Does it look like the swelling is going down?

LEWIS. No.

MILLIE. I didn't know you loved this house so much.

LEWIS. I didn't know I did either.

MILLIE. This house stopped being home when Mom died.

LEWIS. This home is our shelter from the storm.

>   *(The roof leaks.)*

MILLIE. Lewis, I think this old house is just holding us back.

LEWIS. Do you know what happens to people that have no roots?

They float off into space and disappear.

>   (**LEWIS** *marches off.)*

MILLIE. Oh yeah? Well, I'm too fat to float away. And I'll always be rooted to you.

Scene Three – France, 1700s

(**EMILIE** *is at her desk. She is nine months pregnant.* **VOLTAIRE** *enters furious.* **EMILIE** *is huffing and puffing and very pregnant during this fight.*)

VOLTAIRE. Emilie, how can you think yourself a serious woman of science and then give me this paper to read? You cannot send this to the Academie.

EMILIE. I am serious and it is science.

VOLTAIRE. Do you know what you are saying?

EMILIE. When two forces collide...I don't think they cancel each other out.

VOLTAIRE. How can you contradict Newton?

EMILIE. I'm not contradicting –

VOLTAIRE. Your arrogance is appalling!

EMILIE. It's in the numbers.

VOLTAIRE. The numbers don't count.

EMILIE. Gottfried Leibniz thinks the same way.

VOLTAIRE. Gottfried Leibniz is German. Oh, don't even get me started on the Germans.

EMILIE. Voltaire, when energy collides with energy, they don't just cease.

VOLTAIRE. When arrogance collides with naïveté, let me assure you, it risks canceling everything we are doing.

EMILIE. These are equations. Not moral judgments.

VOLTAIRE. All the work we are doing to prove that the universe is based on rational mathematical laws and now you want to cast doubt on Newton's theories?

EMILIE. My equations are correct.

VOLTAIRE. Correct isn't always what's right.

EMILIE. I am not a philosopher! I am a scientist! Argh.

VOLTAIRE. Are you all right?

EMILIE. It's too hot and I'm too fat to be fighting like this.

VOLTAIRE. Then stop working. You have to take care of yourself.

EMILIE. I have to stay awake. There are pages and pages left to do.

VOLTAIRE. You worry about your health and then do nothing to protect it? It's as if you are trying to make your prediction come true! You owe it to yourself, to this child...to me...to lie down and rest.

EMILIE. I just thought I would have more time. When the children were young, I remember thinking, when I am older, I will have time to read all the books and think all the thoughts and know what I do not know and make a contribution to the world that is singular and unique and mine. I know that is folly to think about... I know I mustn't think that way: who am I to assume that I have anything to contribute, but I do.

VOLTAIRE. But you have your children.

EMILIE. And I love them! But they are not me.

VOLTAIRE. And this work is...you?

EMILIE. Tell me Voltaire...if you were given nine months to live what would you do?

Would you rest? Let the ideas in your head go unrecorded? Is that what you would do? Look at me!

VOLTAIRE. *(Beat.)* I would write.

EMILIE. Why would you think it would be different for me?

VOLTAIRE. Emilie, be reasonable.

EMILIE. Be reasonable? I don't have time to be reasonable. I want to be productive!

VOLTAIRE. Emilie.

EMILIE. Being reasonable is for the living! This baby is coming soon.

(Beat.)

VOLTAIRE. What will happen to the child if you die?

EMILIE. Pauline will marry soon...and the baby will go live with her and her new husband. In Italy.

VOLTAIRE. That awful wedding is your idea!

EMILIE. I have to protect the baby.

VOLTAIRE. How could you do this to Pauline?

EMILIE. Do not judge me. You have never had to take care of anybody but yourself.

VOLTAIRE. But Pauline –

EMILIE. Pauline is a clever, resourceful, and generous soul. She will bring this baby into her new household. She will take better care of this child than anyone else I know.

VOLTAIRE. But Pauline is your child.

EMILIE. And she will be an excellent mother.

VOLTAIRE. My goodness...the strategy...and you said nothing.

EMILIE. I am their mother. I have to protect my children.

VOLTAIRE. Any woman can be a mother...you have so much more to offer.

EMILIE. You belittle me and praise me in the same sentence.

VOLTAIRE. It's not just.

EMILIE. It is what it is. Women bear children. And some of us die in the process. It's the natural order.

(Dawning of Illumination...)

VOLTAIRE. No! There is nature, there is chance and there is science. And the reason so many women die in childbirth is because...we let you die.

EMILIE. What?

VOLTAIRE. Think of it, Emilie! Think! The King demands the best cannons...and somehow someway every couple of years, a deadlier one is made. Imagine what would happen if he demanded that doctors find a way to help women survive childbirth?

EMILIE. Voltaire, please don't say that now.

VOLTAIRE. Emilie, this is a matter of conscience. We should go to the King and entreat him! We should go to doctors and demand they prevent your death.

EMILIE. Demand? You are not being reasonable.

VOLTAIRE. "No problem can withstand the assault of sustained thinking".

EMILIE. We can't prevent death.

VOLTAIRE. But we can prolong life if we value it

EMILIE. Voltaire, I no longer fear dying.

VOLTAIRE. But I am afraid of grief.

EMILIE. Don't you realize things happen for a reason? All is for the best in this best of all possible worlds.

(She hugs him and consoles him.)

VOLTAIRE. Oh my dear. You say that with so much faith.

EMILIE. Voltaire, I am going to send this paper to the Academy of Science.

VOLTAIRE. And then you will rest?

EMILIE. Yes, then I will rest.

Scene Four – Experiment Two – Her Discovery

EMILIE. What is energy? For Newton, energy was mass times velocity.

In this equation, in Newton's view...energy disappears. If a carriage hits another carriage...there is a big collision, the energy of each object cancels each other out, and then stillness. Energy is lost forever...and it is in this void, this stillness...where the hand of God enters...intervenes...and reignites the forces that start the world spinning again.

But...if this theory was correct...that would mean that a ball that falls in mud at twice the speed would make a hole twice as deep. But, as Leibniz discovered before me, when a ball falls at twice the speed... the hole it makes in the mud is four times as deep. And if a ball hits the mud at three times the speed... the hole is nine times deeper. Energy is mass times velocity squared...In this view, when two carts or... birds or...lovers...collide...there is a big crash...and then perhaps quiet...but no real stillness...all the energy that brought them into collision gets thrown into the atmosphere in a messy jangle of bent metal and torn wings and broken hearts...vibrating, wringing, beating in new forms of existence. Energy does not escape, it penetrates and transforms. There are no voids. God oversees His creation, but He does not intervene to set things in motion again

Everything changes but nothing is lost. Ever.

   (Lights out.)

Scene Five

> (**MILLIE** *is madly cleaning her house. She is also scooping dirt out of a flower plant and eating it. She is eight and half months pregnant.*)

OLIVIA. Millie, I'm here.

> (**MILLIE** *is dusting listening to music on her earphones.*)

Millie? The door was open.

MILLIE. Oh, you are here early.

OLIVIA. Never late again! Peter is parking the car.

MILLIE. So this is it! Our old house.

OLIVIA. It's charming!

MILLIE. If you say so. Thanks so much for coming by and giving me the ride.

OLIVIA. Of course. We are in for a treat. I looked all over the internet and Urban Moms said this La Maze course was the most satisfying and enriching class in the Tri-State area.

MILLIE. Great. What's all that?

OLIVIA. *What To Expect When You Are Expecting, The Girlfriend's Guide To Babies, The Baby Whisperer*. I'm devouring all of them.

Do you want to borrow some?

MILLIE. No thank you. I don't feel like reading.

OLIVIA. How do you feel?

MILLIE. Like a hippo that ate a whale...I can hear myself breathe when I go up the stairs... Look at me! Can you believe it!? This baby is coming soon. But I have so much I need to do. See? I'm cleaning.

OLIVIA. Oh, I read about that! It's called –

MILLIE & OLIVIA. Nesting.

OLIVIA. Fascinating. Nesting. Incredible how our biology activates deep psychological impulses. Bears and Birds and Bees and humans.

MILLIE. Yeah, I didn't believe it would happen to me...but look at this place. It hasn't looked like nice since Mom lived here. I mean even Lewis is going to be happy about this.

OLIVIA. Come here.

> (**OLIVIA** *absentmindedly does the spit on the finger wipe the kid face move.*)

You have dirt on your face.

MILLIE. I feel very driven to clean.

OLIVIA. And it's good for everyone. Nobody likes dirt, right?

MILLIE. Right. *(Beat.)* Oh the baby just kicked! Feel it?

OLIVIA. Feel what?

MILLIE. The foot...it's up against my belly.

> (**MILLIE** *grabs* **OLIVIA** *hand and places it on her belly.*)

OLIVIA. I don't feel anything.

MILLIE. Wait a second. Ah-ha! There it goes! The kick. Did you feel it!

> (*Suddenly* **OLIVIA** *is uncomfortable.*)

OLIVIA. Oh yes. That's definitely a kicking baby.

MILLIE. Ha! Oh, I have something else I want to show you. *(She brings out a bag.)* Look. I made a little dressing gown for the baby today. Isn't it sweet?

OLIVIA. Oh. It is! So little.

MILLIE. So Soft. All yellow and green. You know because...we don't know...the sex yet.

> (**MILLIE** *strokes the clothes and then slides them over to* **OLIVIA**.)

Here you should take this home. It's for you.

OLIVIA. I love it. Thank you. And don't worry. I'll write you a check for whatever costs you incur for the baby.

MILLIE. OK.

> (**MILLIE** *tears up a little.*)

OLIVIA. Millie, I'm sorry. Did I say something wrong?

MILLIE. No.

OLIVIA. I see all the changes you are going through, and I want to make it easier for you. I so appreciate everything you are doing. You need to spend your money on yourself. On your dreams.

MILLIE. My dreams. Yeah, I know.

OLIVIA. I love the maternity dress.

MILLIE. I made it.

OLIVIA. Please do not feel bad.

MILLIE. Oh, I don't feel bad. I just feel...so much.

OLIVIA. You do?

MILLIE. I'm dusting and everything is a little fuzzy, except that corner of that table...suddenly glares like the really dangerous baby assault weapon that it is.

OLIVIA. Natural instinct is a very compelling force.

MILLIE. Fight or Flight, right?

OLIVIA. Right.

(**MILLIE** *rubs her belly.*)

MILLIE. It's amazingly amazing. I feel so...here. Everything is just so painful and deliciously alive.

(**OLIVIA** *suddenly plops down.*)

Are you OK?

OLIVIA. Yes, I just got a little dizzy.

(**PETER** *comes in.*)

PETER. Oh what a great old house, Millie. All right ladies? Are we ready for the Lamaze? Are you OK?

OLIVIA. I'm all right. Let's go.

(*They all get up to go.* **LEWIS** *walks in. There is a Pause.*)

PETER. Hello, you must be Lewis.

LEWIS. That's right.

OLIVIA. I'm Doctor Olivia Hasting Brown and this is –

PETER. I'm Peter Brown.

(**LEWIS** *punches* **PETER** *in the face.*)

LEWIS. HA!

MILLIE. Lewis!

LEWIS. That felt so good!

PETER. Oh My God.

MILLIE. Oh my God.

OLIVIA. Oh my God.

MILLIE. Lewis!

LEWIS. That felt so good.

OLIVIA. Peter!

LEWIS. That's for taking advantage of my little sister!

MILLIE. Lewis, what's wrong with you!

LEWIS. Wrong with me?

PETER. Lewis, I understand...

LEWIS. No. You can't use my family like this.

OLIVIA. Lewis –

LEWIS. This family is not that kind of family!

MILLIE. Lewis, this is my body and it's their child. Period.

OLIVIA. I think your sister is incredibly resourceful, and sees this as moral, spiritual win-win situation for all of us. We get to build a loving family. And she gets to go to fashion school in Paris.

LEWIS. That's very romantic. Millie, tell them what you are using the money for. Tell them!

PETER. Millie...

LEWIS. Millie is not going to fashion design school. She's not going to Paris. She used all the money to stave off the foreclosure of this house so that she and I won't end up on the street.

(*Beat.*)

PETER. Good God.

MILLIE. I don't see this the same way as Lewis does. I wanted to do something that matters.

LEWIS. Olivia, why can't you have your own baby?

OLIVIA. I had cancer.

PETER. But it's gone.

LEWIS. I'm sorry. What if the cancer comes back?

OLIVIA. It won't.

LEWIS. You can't control that. It might. And I hear if it does it's really fast and really, really bad.

MILLIE. Lewis, stop it. You are being cruel.

LEWIS. Listen, what kind of a crazy person buys a baby when they were just on the brink of dying? It's irrational and irresponsible! Millie, what happens to your baby if she dies?

MILLIE. Oh God.

OLIVIA. Peter is a wonderful care giver. Peter will take better care of this child than anyone I know. He would be an amazing single parent.

PETER. Oh, God.

MILLIE. He will! Peter is the best! Peter will be a much better parent than any of us.

OLIVIA. Oh, God.

MILLIE. Olivia, I'm sorry. I didn't mean you...

OLIVIA. Yes you did. *(Beat.)* And you are absolutely right. *(Pause.)* Lewis is right. This is crazy. And irresponsible. I shouldn't be doing this.

PETER. What?

OLIVIA. I don't feel any of this! All these intense feelings you both are feeling. I DO NOT FEEL.

MILLIE. Of course you do.

OLIVIA. I know I'm supposed to be connected. Intellectually I know that baby contractually belongs to me...and I really love the baby...in my mind...as an idea...but I DO NOT FEEL IT.

LEWIS. Oh no.

PETER. Olivia...

OLIVIA. I'm sorry.

LEWIS. Oh shit!

OLIVIA. I'm sorry. I can't handle this. It's just too much. I need to get out of here!

(And she runs out of there.)

LEWIS. I am the world's worst brother.

PETER. I've never seen Olivia like that. Ever.

LEWIS. What have I done? What are we going to do?

MILLIE. Lewis, please shut up. I've had enough out of you. Peter, go that way. I'll go this way. Lewis, stay here and do nothing. We have to find Olivia. Bring umbrellas. It looks like it's going to rain.

Scene Six – France 1700s

(**VOLTAIRE** *is pacing. We hear the sounds of* **EMILIE** *in labor in the room. We hear the baby cry.* **VOLTAIRE** *can't take it anymore and bursts in the room.*)

VOLTAIRE. EMILIE!

EMILIE. It's a girl. A beautiful little girl.

VOLTAIRE. You look so well!

EMILIE. I feel so well! Look at her, Voltaire, she's perfect.

VOLTAIRE. Just like her mother.

EMILIE. So little.

VOLTAIRE. She will grow!

EMILIE. She's so sweet. My heart aches just looking at her.

VOLTAIRE. You need to rest.

EMILIE. Look at her hands – so strong and small.

VOLTAIRE. You are beautiful.

EMILIE. Do you want to hold her?

VOLTAIRE. Oh! I've never held someone so tiny. (*He takes her.*)

EMILIE. Hold her head...

VOLTAIRE. Her eyes... Oh! She just opened her eyes...for a second.

EMILIE. Hello little girl. I'm your mother. And this is...

VOLTAIRE. Uncle Voltaire. Oh! There! She did it again! She opened her eyes!

EMILIE. Oh, let me see!

VOLTAIRE. Her lips are a perfect letter "O."

PAULINE. Maman.

> (**PAULINE** *enters her stunning wedding dress...full of stars.*)

EMILIE. Pauline!

PAULINE. For the wedding next week. I wanted you to see me.

EMILIE. You are a beautiful bride, Pauline

PAULINE. Thank you.

EMILIE. But you will not marry Duke Fabio Montenaro next week.

PAULINE. *Maman...*

EMILIE. You belong here, at home, with me and your sister. And your brother will return from the army. And Voltaire will write. Jean François will visit. You will wear that gown in the salons of Paris. We will demand entry to the university. We will be happy.

> (**THE WET NURSE** *enters. It is* **OLIVIA** *with a full healthy bosom...dressed as a peasant...ready to feed a baby that is not hers.*)

VOLTAIRE. The wet nurse is here.

WET NURSE. Madame, you look so –

EMILIE. Well?

WET NURSE. Wonderful!

VOLTAIRE. Doesn't she? I love it when you are wrong!

EMILIE. Today, I love being wrong too.

WET NURSE. The baby is small.

EMILIE. The baby is perfect.

WET NURSE. Allow me to feed her, *Madame.*

(**EMILIE** *refuses to let the baby go.*)

EMILIE. Not yet.

PAULINE. The baby needs to eat, *Maman.*

EMILIE. But then this perfect moment will pass. Let me hold her. I can feed her.

WET NURSE. Madame...No. It wouldn't be proper. It is my work.

EMILIE. Where is Jean-François? Why is he not here yet?

VOLTAIRE. He doesn't deserve to father someone so bright and delicate.

EMILIE. Voltaire, you must promise not to fight with Jean-François.

PAULINE. *Maman...*Let me hold the baby.

EMILIE. Be careful.

PAULINE. Hello little girl.

(**EMILIE** *hands the baby to her daughter.*)

EMILIE. You were just as small...and look at you now.

PAULINE. Yes, look at me now.

EMILIE. As bright as the night sky. I look at the two of you...and I feel...immortal.

PAULINE. *(Tenderly strokes her Mother's cheek.) Maman,* rest.

(**PAULINE** *hands the baby to the* **WET NURSE.** *The* **WET NURSE** *feeds the baby.*)

WET NURSE. *(To the baby.) Viens ici, ma petite. Oui, c'est comme ça.*

(*She clucks as the baby nurses, like it's the most natural thing in the world.*)

EMILIE. It's so hot... I'm so tired...

VOLTAIRE. It is August.

EMILIE. And I am alive!

> (**THE WET NURSE** *and* **EMILIE** *sing a lullaby in French underneath the following**.)

DODO L'ENFANT DO
L'ENFANT DORMIRA BIEN VITE
DODO L'ENFANT DO
L'ENFANT DORMIRA BIENTÔT

> (**THE WET NURSE** *feeds the baby. Then* **PAULINE** *gently helps* **EMILIE** *up and they slowly exit...***THE WET NURSE** *leading the way, holding the baby, while* **PAULINE** *helps* **EMILIE.** **VOLTAIRE** *watches them all go. He is alone.*)

VOLTAIRE. A few days later, Emilie died,

from an infection after the birth of her child. Her infant daughter Adelaide lived a little longer, and then, also succumbed.

Pauline married the old Duke in Italy.

Marquis du Châtelet never remarried.

Emilie's only son Louis was guillotined during the French Revolution...With his death the du Châtelet line ceased.

Emilie's treatise on Newton's *Principia* lingered in obscurity for ten years after her death, until a passing comet ignited people's interest in all things celestial. It was suddenly discovered, dusted off, and published. It is the translation still used in France today.

---

* A license to produce *Legacy of Light* does not include a performance license for any third-party or copyrighted music. Licensees should create an original composition or use music in the public domain. For further information, please see the Music and Third-Party Materials Use Note on page iii.

VOLTAIRE. Twelve years after the death of Emilie, I wrote a short story called entitled *Candide*.

Candide is the story of an optimistic man who accepts every bitter thing life has to offer with the phrase ALL IS FOR THE BEST IN THIS BEST OF ALL POSSIBLE WORLDS.

After it was published, I was banished by the King...and lived the rest of my life in Exile.

I died at the age of eighty-four; I lived twice as long as Emilie.

All is for the Best in this best of all possible worlds.

How Emilie could say that, is...beyond me.

(**VOLTAIRE** *watches* **EMILIE** *and her baby disappear into the dark...and then* **VOLTAIRE** *watches a visibly distraught screaming* **OLIVIA** *run by him and climb up the apple tree.*)

Scene Seven

OLIVIA. Aaaahhh!

VOLTAIRE. Madame, what are you doing up there?

OLIVIA. Oh My God. What is going on! Why is a French man with a white curly wig talking to me???

VOLTAIRE. I am Voltaire.

OLIVIA. What are you doing here in New Jersey? Good God, I am mad.

VOLTAIRE. No, no...you're just a little flustered.

OLIVIA. I am not flustered. I am crazy. I'm up in a tree –

VOLTAIRE. A change of perspective is healthy.

OLIVIA. Talking to Voltaire.

VOLTAIRE. Perhaps New Jersey is a very Enlightened place, *n'est ce pas?*

OLIVIA. Why can I understand the universe and not something as simple as a baby?

VOLTAIRE. You understand the universe?

OLIVIA. It's whirling and expanding as we speak!

VOLTAIRE. *(Grabs on tight.)* It is?

OLIVIA. Don't you feel it?

VOLTAIRE. Not really.

OLIVIA. That's because of gravity.

VOLTAIRE. Oh! I understand gravity! But how can the universe be expanding? I thought it was like a clock.

OLIVIA. It's a little messier than that.

VOLTAIRE. Is Newton wrong?

OLIVIA. No, but he just isn't right all the time. There's room for other theories like special relativity, quantum mechanics, like string theory.

VOLTAIRE. Emilie was right, after all.

OLIVIA. Oh God! Why did I want to be a mother?

VOLTAIRE. It's a common urge.

OLIVIA. Why did I think becoming a mother would make me whole?

VOLTAIRE. From my limited observations, motherhood makes you whole and splits you apart at the same time.

OLIVIA. Did you have children?

VOLTAIRE. No, I did not.

OLIVIA. You were passionate about what you did. You lived your life fully. Look what contributions you were able to make.

VOLTAIRE. Thank you!

OLIVIA. You were the father of the Enlightenment. You came up with the concept of human rights. I read *Candide* in high school.

VOLTAIRE. You are wonderful!

OLIVIA. I have a planet. An embryonic core of a planet that might, in a million years, be a vital part of a different solar system. That might give us clues to how our Earth was formed. And I want to understand it, watch it grow, and hope it will be everything it could possibly be.

VOLTAIRE. We each have our own garden to tend.

OLIVIA. I do! And yet –

VOLTAIRE. Yet?

OLIVIA. The baby is coming anyway.

VOLTAIRE. Oh. Are you...expecting?

OLIVIA. Yes. I'm expecting.

VOLTAIRE. Oh! You are with child?

OLIVIA. Oh, no. But Millie is. I want to understand and to feel...And I try. I want to. I really do. But I look at her huge round belly and her flushed face and I have NO Earthly idea what she is really going through. What kind of mother is that?

VOLTAIRE. *(Beat.)* A father.

> *(Beat.)*

OLIVIA. A father.

VOLTAIRE. There was a child: Pauline. She wasn't mine. But I cut her apple slices; I taught her how to write her name. She made the costumes for my plays. She was a bright ray of light in my life.

OLIVIA. A father.

> *(Raindrops, wind.)*

VOLTAIRE. A storm is coming.

MILLIE. *(Offstage.)* OLIVIA!

OLIVIA. Oh no! It's the Mother. She's coming to get me.

Scene Eight

(**MILLIE** *comes on stage. She is on a mission.*)

MILLIE. Doctor Olivia Hasting Brown!

VOLTAIRE. That's her?

OLIVIA. Yes. The Mother.

VOLTAIRE. She looks familiar.

OLIVIA. I don't want her to see me.

MILLIE. There you are! You think I can't see you. But I do. Come down from that tree immediately young...middle-aged lady!

OLIVIA. I want to be alone.

MILLIE. Well, I have some news for you, Doctor, this is not about what you want.

Your daughter needs you.

OLIVIA. It's a girl?

MILLIE. Yes, it's a girl.

OLIVIA. You found out? When I asked you not to?

MILLIE. I wanted to know.

OLIVIA. And you didn't tell me?

MILLIE. You didn't want to know.

OLIVIA. Right.

MILLIE. I'm sorry I didn't tell you about the house. I was scared you wouldn't choose me.

OLIVIA. Millie, I wouldn't have chosen anyone else but you.

MILLIE. Please come down, Olivia.

OLIVIA. I can't.

MILLIE. Yes, you can.

OLIVIA. I can't. I'm sorry.

> (**MILLIE** *starts shaking the tree.*)

MILLIE. Come down, Olivia.

OLIVIA. I don't know if I can go through with any of this.

> (**MILLIE** *starts to climb the tree.*)

MILLIE. I don't care if I have to come get you. You are coming down that tree.

OLIVIA. Millie, you can't. You're pregnant.

> (**MILLIE** *slides down.*)

MILLIE. Don't tell me what I can and can't do, Doctor Olivia Hasting Brown.

OLIVIA. Stop it, Millie. Think of the baby.

MILLIE. I am thinking of the baby.

> (**MILLIE** *starts to climb again.*)

OLIVIA. Stop climbing!

MILLIE. Olivia! Get down here this instant!

OLIVIA. I'm so sorry.

> (**MILLIE** *throws an apple at* **OLIVIA**.)

No.

MILLIE. You're leaving me like this?

OLIVIA. Millie, I chose you because I knew there was nothing you couldn't handle. You can handle this.

MILLIE. Olivia...You have a tenured position at the Isaac Newton Institute. You have discovered an embryonic core of a planet. You survived late-stage ovarian cancer.

OLIVIA. So?

MILLIE. Parenthood isn't rocket science.

OLIVIA. Exactly! My Mom, she picked me up from school every single day. I always had matching socks and clean underwear. Saturday, she drove me to violin. But I don't know what she thought. I don't know how she felt.

MILLIE. This is your baby.

OLIVIA. Prove it!

MILLIE. Ohmigod, you aren't going to come down are you?

OLIVIA. That baby will be the most wonderful thing that ever happened to you.

MILLIE. Ohmigod.

OLIVIA. All is for the best in this best of all possible worlds.

VOLTAIRE. Don't say that.

MILLIE. Oh. I miss my Mom.

OLIVIA. Oh Millie.

MILLIE. (**MILLIE** *sinks to the ground.*) I wish she was here.

OLIVIA. (**OLIVIA** *starts to descend.*) It will be all right.

MILLIE. I really, really miss her.

OLIVIA. (**OLIVIA** *gets to* **MILLIE** *and hugs her.*) There. There.

MILLIE. Oh.

OLIVIA. Oh.

Shh.

Oh.

MILLIE. Oh.

OLIVIA. Oh.

MILLIE. Oh-oh.

OLIVIA. What?

MILLIE. I'm wet. My water broke!

OLIVIA. *(To* **VOLTAIRE.***)* I have to get her to a hospital.

VOLTAIRE. I can't go through this again

> (**MILLIE** *is in full labor. The storm gets stronger.*)

OLIVIA. Hold on Millie. Don't worry. I'll make sure you and the baby are both going to be just fine.

> (**MILLIE** *and* **OLIVIA** *exit.* **VOLTAIRE** *remains up in the tree.*)

EMILIE. Voltaire, you should come down from there. It's raining.

VOLTAIRE. Emilie, it's you.

EMILIE. *Oui. C'est moi.*

VOLTAIRE. You are luminous.

EMILIE. It's still me.

VOLTAIRE. The night you died, I wrote a poem "I shall await you quietly – in my meridian, in the fields of Cirey. Watching one star only. Watching my Emilie."

EMILIE. That is beautiful.

VOLTAIRE. Thirty years I had to live without you. And I missed you everyday. I lived eighty-four years and found only one truth: that flies were born to be devoured by spiders, and men to be consumed by sorrow.

EMILIE. Oh, *Mon Cher* Voltaire. "To enjoy life, we must touch much of it lightly".

PETER. *(Offstage.)* Olivia! Olivia!

VOLTAIRE. Who's that?

EMILIE. I don't know.

Scene Nine

> (**PETER** *is out looking for* **OLIVIA**. *A bad storm is coming. It is raining. It is windy. We hear thunder. He is calling out for* **OLIVIA**. **VOLTAIRE** *watches from his tree.*)

PETER. Olivia! Where are you? You have to get back to the house. It's not safe out here.

> (*A flash of lightening hits* **PETER** *instantly. Maybe hundreds of apples fall out of trees. And* **PETER** *dies.* **EMILIE** *enters.*)

EMILIE. You just got struck by lightning!

PETER. Oh no...

EMILIE. How did it feel?

PETER. Like I got hit by a cannon ball. Like...like...I just died. *(Beat.)* It's all over. And I didn't even see it coming. Am I dead?

EMILIE. I am sorry.

PETER. I never asked for much. I never had grand designs. I tend my own garden. I go to the supermarket. I teach writing. I buy small pencils. I'm just a man who goes to work. I'm just a man who loves his wife.

EMILIE. I know.

PETER. But God! I'm not going to see Olivia again. I'm not going to meet our baby.

EMILIE. I'm so sorry.

PETER. I do not want to be dead.

EMILIE. *(Places her hands on his chest.)* Your heart has stopped.

PETER. Hit it.

EMILIE. Hit your heart?

> (**PETER** *grabs her hands and pumps them*
> *against his chest.*)

PETER. With all your might.

EMILIE. But...

PETER. Harder. Again.

EMILIE. Like this?

PETER. Help me!

EMILIE. More?

PETER. Again!

EMILIE. I'm trying. Is it working? Oh! Oh! Oh!

> (*He rises to his feet.*)

PETER. Yes!

EMILIE. It's a miracle!

PETER. It's science!

EMILIE. Monsieur, you are one of those people that are hit
by light and to live to tell about it.

PETER. Where there is a will, sometimes, there is a way.
And I have so much I need to do. Olivia! Olivia!

> (**PETER** *exits.* **EMILIE** *is all breathless and*
> *flustered by what has just happened.*
> **VOLTAIRE** *comes down the tree.*)

EMILIE. Voltaire, did you see that?

VOLTAIRE. Simply incredible how you still manage to get
a rise out of men.

EMILIE. Voltaire, it's just like Newton said: an unmoving
object will not move unless a force acts upon it.

SAINT LAMBERT. *(Off stage.)* Emilie!

EMILIE. It's Jean-François!

VOLTAIRE. Wait! He can't see you.

EMILIE. Why not?

VOLTAIRE. Emilie, he doesn't know yet.

ST. LAMBERT. Emilie, it's me.

EMILIE. Doesn't know what?

VOLTAIRE. That you died. Go!

       (**EMILIE** *hides.* **VOLTAIRE** *faces* **ST. LAMBERT.**)

SAINT-LAMBERT. I'm here to see Emilie.

VOLTAIRE. Saint-Lambert, finally here, are you?

SAINT-LAMBERT. I meant to come sooner...but...

VOLTAIRE. But...

SAINT LAMBERT. The King, who is very displeased with you, has asked me to try to capture the very moment summer greens mature into vibrant autumn foliage. And my vigil is constant, since the trees are due to turn any moment.

CHÂTELET. *(Entering.)* Who is this?

VOLTAIRE. Marquis du Châtelet...This is Saint-Lambert.

CHÂTELET. I wish I could say I was pleased to meet you, but I am not.

SAINT LAMBERT. I am here to see Emilie and my – the – child.

CHÂTELET. Did you not receive the news?

SAINT-LAMBERT. What news?

CHÂTELET. Emilie is dead. And so is your child.

SAINT LAMBERT. I received her joyous letter that all was well.

VOLTAIRE. Everything changed.

CHÂTELET. She asked for you...she wanted to see you.

VOLTAIRE. For days, she asked for you.

SAINT-LAMBERT. Marquis, Voltaire, you must understand the King asked me to stay. *(Beat.)* I thought all was well!

CHÂTELET. Excuse me, Saint Lambert because I am an older man...raised in old fashioned ways...but I do feel the need to express this sentiment to you.

SAINT-LAMBERT. Marquis?

> (**CHÂTELET** *swings his fist and hits* **SAINT-LAMBERT** *on the nose.*)

CHÂTELET. Every action has an equal and opposite reaction.

SAINT LAMBERT. Oh my God. Oh my God. Oh my God.

> (**CHÂTELET** *and* **VOLTAIRE** *bow to each other.* **CHÂTELET** *exits.* **VOLTAIRE** *grabs* **ST. LAMBERT**...*helps him up, brusquely.*)

VOLTAIRE. I have never made but one prayer to God...a very short one "O Lord, make my enemies ridiculous. And God granted it."

SAINT-LAMBERT. She's gone. And the baby. Gone...

VOLTAIRE. *(To the audience.)* Everyone, this is Jean-François de Saint Lambert...the silly puppy who did not pay attention and killed Emilie du Châtelet.

SAINT-LAMBERT. *(Falls apart.)* I loved Emilie. I did. I loved her.

VOLTAIRE. Every man is guilty of all the good he did not do.

> (**VOLTAIRE** *slams the door on him.* **EMILIE** *tries to run after him.*)

EMILIE. Jean-François, wait!

> (**VOLTAIRE** *stops her from going after* **ST. LAMBERT**.)

You were horrible to him.

VOLTAIRE. That silly little puppy. He deserved it.

EMILIE. He is devastated.

VOLTAIRE. He was not the only one.

EMILIE. He loved me. He was so happy about the baby.

VOLTAIRE. He abandoned you.

EMILIE. He was at Court!

VOLTAIRE. He is the reason you died. You would not have died if you had not loved him.

EMILIE. His love did not kill me.

VOLTAIRE. No, I did.

EMILIE. That is irrational.

VOLTAIRE. Those other women! Those stupid letters I wrote.

EMILIE. Voltaire, I chose to love St. Lambert.

VOLTAIRE. How could I know things would end up like this?

EMILIE. You couldn't. *C'est-LA-VIE*!

> (**LEWIS** *runs on.*)

LEWIS. You! You speak French.

VOLTAIRE & EMILIE. *Mais oui.*

LEWIS. I'm not the sort of brother that would usually consider opening a letter like this, but life has been very chaotic, and I can't make sense of it all. There's been too much change. My mother died –

EMILIE. I'm sorry. You look so familiar.

LEWIS. And my sister is pregnant. With this school teacher Peter...who is married to a woman named Olivia.

EMILIE. So, your sister is Peter's mistress?

LEWIS. No. No. She's involved with both of them.

VOLTAIRE. *A ménage-a-trois?*

LEWIS. No! God No! How can I explain it? They have paid her to have Peter's baby.

VOLTAIRE. They paid your sister *to faire l'amour* with the husband?

LEWIS. No! She conceived the husband's baby, but there was *no fairing l'amouring.*

EMILIE. There was no lovemaking?

VOLTAIRE. And this is progress?

LEWIS. She is giving birth to the child but she will not be the mother. Anyway, Millie is so young, only twenty-one, and pregnant.

VOLTAIRE. You are concerned she will die during childbirth.

LEWIS. Oh God! Should I be?

EMILIE. It happens. Why is your sister doing this?

LEWIS. Olivia was supposed to die but she didn't. Then she discovered a planet and wanted a baby, that my sister is having so she can pay to go to school in Paris but instead she used all the money to save my mother's house.

VOLTAIRE. Amazing how much Americans reveal about themselves to complete strangers.

LEWIS. Except, now today, a letter came in the mail. From Paris. For Millie. From the Grand E-colee. And it could change everything. Would you please read it and translate it for me?

> *(He hands the unopened letter to* **EMILIE.***)*

EMILIE. *(Looks at the envelope.)* Emilia Montenaro. Emilia Montenaro?

VOLTAIRE. Are you Italian?

LEWIS. Through my Mom.

EMILIE. What is your name?

LEWIS. Lewis Fabio Montenaro.

> *(***EMILIE** *hugs* **LEWIS.***)*

EMILIE. Oh my! You sweet, sweet boy! Now, I have to find your sister.

> *(***EMILIE** *hands* **LEWIS** *the unopened envelope and runs off.* **LEWIS** *looks at the letter and then at* **VOLTAIRE.***)*

LEWIS. What should we do?

VOLTAIRE. It is dangerous to read letters not meant for you.

> *(***LEWIS** *nods and puts the letter in his back pocket.)*

LEWIS. Do lots of people in France dress like you?

VOLTAIRE. *(Beat.)* Yes. They do.

Scene Ten – New Jersey – Now

*(At the threshold of the hospital. They are leaving the hospital. **PETER** has gone for the car. **MILLIE** is holding the baby. **OLIVIA** is holding **MILLIE**'s luggage and a bouquet of flowers with a pink helium balloon that reads "It's a BABY.")*

*(**MILLIE** holds the baby. Sings the same beautiful lullaby...in Italian "Dare La Lucce.")*

MILLIE.

> DORME BAMBINO
> DORME BAMBINO ADESSO
> DORME BAMBINO
> BIMBO DORMIRA FRA PO

OLIVIA. She's so little.

MILLIE. Yes.

OLIVIA. She doesn't look like Peter very much.

MILLIE. Not yet.

OLIVIA. You were amazingly amazing in there.

MILLIE. It was more intense than I expected.

OLIVIA. It's not called labor for nothing.

MILLIE. I can't believe that it's all over!

OLIVIA. Me neither.

MILLIE. You and baby Agnes are going home today.

---

*A license to produce *Legacy of Light* does not include a performance license for any third-party or copyrighted music. Licensees should create an original composition or use music in the public domain. For further information, please see the Music and Third-Party Materials Use Note on page iii.

OLIVIA. You know what? Agnes is really not the right name for her.

MILLIE. Oh, I'm so glad you said that. Do you have another name in mind?

OLIVIA. I think our daughter should live with the name you choose to give her.

MILLIE. Me? Really?

OLIVIA. I think so.

MILLIE. I get to choose. Oh! I know what I want! I want to name her Pauline. It was my mother's name. It's been a family name for generations.

> (**MILLIE** *kisses the baby's forehead hands* **OLIVIA** *the sleeping baby.*)

OLIVIA. That's perfect. Hello sweet Pauline, I am your mother.

> *(The baby starts to cry.)*

OLIVIA. Oh no.

MILLIE. It's OK.

OLIVIA. Your Daddy will be here any second. He'll know how to make you happy.

MILLIE. Shhh, baby...

OLIVIA. I can't do this, Millie. Where's Peter? I can't.

MILLIE. Yes you can. Here sing something that's you.

(Olivia sings a popular rock and roll song about science...like the one by Thomas Dolby...or one by Sam Cooke...*)

(The baby sleeps. **PETER**, *with a bandage on his nose, enters with a car seat.)*

PETER. I've got the car. Oh, look at her! Her lips are a perfect letter "O."

OLIVIA. Peter...what do you think of the name... Pauline?

PETER. Perfect! Hello, little Pauline Brown.

OLIVIA. Okay now be careful.

(They put the baby in the car seat.)

PETER. You have to have a PhD to snap that in.

*(**OLIVIA** snaps the baby in.)*

OLIVIA. Cover her up. Where's the pacifier?

PETER. I don't think she needs a pacifier. Does her head look okay?

OLIVIA. Fixes something.

I think that's better.

(Time to say goodbye.)

PETER. OK.

---

* A license to produce *Legacy of Light* does not include a performance license for a Thomas Dolby or Sam Cooke song. The publisher and author suggest that the licensee contact ASCAP or BMI to ascertain the music publisher and contact such music publisher to license or acquire permission for performance of the song. If a license or permission is unattainable for a Thomas Dolby or Sam Cooke song, the licensee may not use the song in *Legacy of Light* but should create an original composition in a similar style or use a similar song in the public domain. For further information, please see the Music and Third-Party Materials Use Note on page iii.

OLIVIA. OK.

MILLIE. OK.

PETER. Is Lewis coming to get you?

MILLIE. Yes... I think he's just waiting for you to leave. You know, he feels bad about your nose.

OLIVIA. Millie –

MILLIE. The pleasure was all mine. I can't tell you how happy I am to see you this happy.

> *(They hug her.)*

OLIVIA. The diaper bag! Who has the diaper bag?

MILLIE. Here.

PETER. The application for the birth certificate! Where did I put it?

MILLIE. It's in a folder in the diaper bag.

OLIVIA. You need to come visit us very soon.

MILLIE. Of course.

OLIVIA. Careful, Peter, she's a baby, not a fruit basket!

> **(PETER** *exits with the baby and flowers and balloon.)*

Millie? **(MILLIE** *turns around.)*

You will always be her mother.

MILLIE. So will you, Olivia.

OLIVIA. Thank you.

> **(OLIVIA** *exit.* **MILLIE** *sits on her suitcase and waits.)*
>
> **(LEWIS** *runs in with flowers.)*

LEWIS. I parked way out of the way. So they wouldn't see me. But I wanted to let you know I am here.

MILLIE. Thank you.

LEWIS. How do you feel?

MILLIE. Good. Tired. Happy. Sad.

LEWIS. Here. I have something for you.

> (**LEWIS** *gives her a quick hug and some flowers.*)

MILLIE. You hate flowers.

LEWIS. But you don't. Stay put, sis. I'm going to get the car.

> (*He starts to exit, reconsiders and comes back.*)

Also, this letter came in the mail for you today.

> (*He hands her the rumpled, unopened letter.*)

Why didn't you tell me you actually applied?

MILLIE. I didn't think it would matter.

LEWIS. Yeah! It does.

> (*He exits.*)

> (**MILLIE** *sits on the suitcase. She is alone. She looks at the letter and then she begins to weep.*)

Scene Eleven

(**EMILIE** *appears.*)

EMILIE. Emilia!

MILLIE. Mom?

EMILIE. No.

MILLIE. Only my mom called me Emilia. *(She wipes her eyes.)* Everyone else calls me Millie. Wow, your dress is amazingly amazing.

EMILIE. Merci. Merci beaucoup. Are you going to open the letter?

MILLIE. It's from Paris...

EMILIE. You should open it.

MILLIE. I don't want to know what's inside. I'm scared. Maybe they don't want me.

EMILIE. Maybe they do.

MILLIE. I can't go. I have nothing. I used all the money to save the house.

EMILIE. A friend of mine used to say "No problem can withstand the assault of sustained thinking."

MILLIE. That's optimistic.

EMILIE. My daughter always dreamed of going to Paris. Open the letter, Emilia.

(**MILLIE** *opens the letter and reads it!*)

MILLIE. Oh no.

EMILIE. What?

MILLIE. *(Beat.)* I got in. I got in! I GOT IN!

> (**MILLIE** *and* **EMILIE** *hug excitedly like a Mom and child would.*)

What shall I do?

EMILIE. Find a way to get there.

MILLIE. I'll get more hours at the Library. Maybe they have a scholarship. Maybe Olivia and Peter have an idea. I'll talk to Lewis. Maybe we will sell the house. Or rent it. (**MILLIE** *picks up her suitcase, lost in her planning.*)

EMILIE. Emilia?

MILLIE. Yes?

> (**EMILIE** *strokes* **MILLIE**'s *cheek.*)

EMILIE. I look at you and I feel immortal.

> (**EMILIE** *plucks an apple and hands it to* **MILLIE.**)

Always do something that matters.

> (*The apple glows like a light.*)

MILLIE. Merci. Merci beaucoup.

> (**MILLIE** *picks up the suitcase and leaves with joyful resolve.*)

EMILIE. She looks so much like my Pauline.

> (**VOLTAIRE** *comes forward.*)

VOLTAIRE. The apple does not fall far from the tree.

EMILIE. Look at her go.

VOLTAIRE. She is light.

EMILIE. Oh Voltaire...She is energy!

> (*She smiles at him, they kiss.*)

EMILIE. Everything changes, but nothing is lost. Ever.

(Stars illuminate...everywhere.)

The End

Printed in the USA
CPSIA information can be obtained
at www.ICGtesting.com
JSHW061812151024
71761JS00022B/634